D1186660

B. Monkey

Andrew Davies
B. MONKEY

LONDON TORONTO

First published in Great Britain 1992
by Lime Tree
an imprint of the Octopus Publishing Group
Michelin House, 81 Fulham Road, London SW3 6RB

A CIP catalogue record for this book
is available from the British Library
ISBN 0 413 63660 7

Printed in England
by Clays Ltd, St. Ives PLC

Lyrics from 'They Can't Take That Away From Me'
© 1937 Gershwin Pub Corp, USA
Chappell Music Ltd/International Music Publications
are used by permission .

A

Waking in the mornings, taking such pleasure in watching her sleep. I always wake early. Sometimes I have this . . . hollow papery feeling. Watching her sleep makes me better. She sleeps very still and quiet. On her front with her bottom in the air like a baby. On her back with one hand flung back behind her head, her hand open, her fingers slightly curled, her arm completely relaxed as if she were anaesthetised, the little dark ringlet of hair in her armpit sort of . . . sweet and defenceless-looking. On her side facing me breathing quietly into my face. On her side facing away from me, the smooth skin on her back looking almost translucent: if I move so that my belly's touching her she'll push back against me in her sleep and reach for me with the back of her thighs until she's in effect sitting on my lap. She'll curl her strong toes around my toes and hold them in her sleep. She loves me in her sleep.

B. Monkey.

Beatrice.

I love her so much I think it might be bad for me.

To tell the truth, though – and I want to tell the truth because I cannot bear deception – it's not always like that. Quite a few times I've woken up and she hasn't been there beside me at all. I'm not talking about seven in the morning or even six, I'm talking about three or four a.m. Bad dream time, shitty panic time. Anyway, these times I'll wrestle up out of sleep with that hollow sick papery feeling, and go looking for her. And find her, usually, curled up in a corner on a heap of cushions with the spare duvet over her, fast asleep like that. I don't know if she sleepwalks there or what, she doesn't seem too clear about that herself. Sometimes I get her to come back into bed, sometimes I leave her. A couple of times, I got the feeling she wouldn't mind me creeping into her little nest with her, so I did that and held her in my arms till it was light.

Secrets of marriage.

I just don't know whether that sort of thing is normal behaviour or not. I don't care, really. It seems all right to me.

She has always said that I can ask her any question I like, and she won't mind, but that I must try not to mind if sometimes she doesn't want to answer.

Mostly she answers.

Mostly she answers so fully, so . . . fearlessly, opening up her thoughts and her feelings the same way she opens her body to me, I've found myself listening to things that astonished me, sometimes, and sometimes things I found a bit difficult to handle. But it can be exciting to ask so little and be told so much. There was a time when I got hooked on asking her questions; I thought if I kept asking I would know not only everything there was to know about her, but everything there was to know about being a woman, really . . . silly. You can never know everything, can you?

And there have been times when I've asked her something, and she's just smiled, or looked at me thoughtfully, and not answered.

And a few times, just a few times, when I've woken at three or four with the hollow papery feeling and gone looking for her in the corners of the rooms, and been unable to find her.

I don't know where she goes at those times, or who she sees, or what she does.

I understand that I have to trust her.

B

What it is, I feel is if he smothers the fuck out of me sometimes, not always, just sometimes, he's just so sort of steady and good and it rattles me, I don't think I shall ever quite get used to it, not being steady and good myself in fact far from it, being in fact a bit of a case. What it is, I want to change, and I have, but not entirely, I don't think you ever do, quite, and anyway, I think it might be what appeals, partly.

My being a bit of wild.

I feel so safe with him.

Too safe, sometimes.

That's all.

But that's where the rain gets in.

A

The first time I saw her was down the gym. She was there with two boys, one of them a little Greek-looking bodybuilder type, the other one a tall skinny Black kid. Not literally black, of course, in fact far from it, he was very light-coloured. I thought they all looked about seventeen or eighteen. They were doing sets on the Nautilus machines. They were laughing a lot, and I thought they seemed very close, like a family. There was something very vivid and bright about all three of them, but especially her. I had never seen them at the gym before, which was odd, because at that time I used to go there every day, and they were treating the place as if they owned it.

Doing sets, in threes, is a typically laddish pursuit and I had never seen a girl involved in it. The way you do it is like this: A straps himself into the machine and pumps iron, egged on by B and C, until temporary muscle failure sets in. Then B, the same, egged on by A and C, then C, then A again, and so on until all three of them are like limp sweat-drenched rags. Then on to the next machine.

She was doing very well, I thought. *Was* that what I thought? Well it was one of the things I was thinking, besides wondering whether she might be the one, and thinking, even then, how tough and wiry she looked and yet at the same time so utterly and desperately in need of someone to love and protect her. She was wearing a pink singlet and black tracksuit bottoms. As she lifted her arms to grasp the thick black pads of foam rubber and cracked plastic and drive them together in front of her face, I could see the outline of her small nipples, and in her armpits the damp ringlets of dark hair, and it's strange and not strange that even then I knew it was all right for me to be looking but I

5

didn't want anyone else to be looking. The thing is, I felt she was already mine, or that I was hers. (Oh, yes, likely tale, son, and how often have you felt like that about a girl idly glimpsed down the gym or down the pool or in the pub or in the street or even waiting for her kids outside the school? About five hundred times? Five million? Fifty? Five? – Yes, all right, fair question. Somewhere between the last two, but nearer the five than the fifty and mostly then just as a sort of dream which would dissolve as soon as she opened her mouth to talk. Yes, I am a very picky person, and no, there's nothing particularly wonderful about me to justify it. For me it was always all or nothing.)

She's there now in my head, her small face framed neatly by the straight back lines of the machine, veins standing out on her neck, sweat dripping off her nose, her mouth half open showing her bright teeth and her sharp red tongue out a little to the side, frowning ferociously, taking great gasps of air as she forces the heavy arms of the machine together in front of her face again and again.

There's that film they show you in the top year in primary school, about love and sex and where the babies come from, and the climax is of course where this woman is giving birth, and the thing about this film that remains in my mind, perhaps even more than the determination of the baby to battle his way out, was the woman's face as she was pushing, the effort there, the strength, the way – no, I couldn't have articulated it then, but I think I did feel it – the way you couldn't separate her and what she was doing, she was what she was doing, yes, that was it, and that was what struck me most about her too, Beatrice I mean, when I first saw her. I had never seen anyone else who gave herself so completely to what she was doing, just *was* in that moment what she was doing – oh body swayed to music, oh brightening glance, how can we tell the dancer from the dance, as my fucking father would no doubt say at this point if he were here, though Christ knows I have never met a human being further from his instincts less capable of living in the moment and more fucked up than that – no, leave that. Leave it. Leave it. Leave it.

The other thing I felt, the word that swam into my head, as I was feasting my eyes on her that day – a total stranger then,

6

how weird that seems now – was the word enthroned. Yes. Something to do with the shape of the machine, of course. Those original black Nautilus machines – all the flasher gyms have upgraded to the second generation model years ago – as frank about themselves as old-fashioned dentist's chairs, showing all their works, functional and ritualistic . . . and then the stiff hieratic gestures they impose: there she sat in her special clothing, performing motions as narrowly prescribed as the motions of a priest or a puppet: her arms spread wide in welcome, then closed in an inviolable circle. Benign and remote. The acolytes crouching at her feet, one brown, one white. Enthroned. Hark at him. Virgin Mary, terrible, yes. This boy is cruising for a bruising, as the kids say now, even the seven-year-olds.

Get on, get on.

I was on one of the bikes pedalling away up and down the random hill sequence on level nine staring at her with I suppose my gob hanging open and suddenly she opened her eyes wide and looked back at me and started to laugh and she lost it, the arms of the machine swung back with a crash spreading her own arms so wide it looked as if her shoulders had dislocated and she let out a yell and then just sat there pinned and shaking with laughter, and every time she looked across at me it seemed to spark off another spasm. By now everyone in the gym was staring at her and some of them were staring at me. I could feel myself going red but it didn't seem to bother her in the least. That should have done it, really, put me off her for good, I mean, that raucous girl-yob thing she had and still has, a little, but it didn't. It was lovely, really. I thought so.

What happened then was that Rupert came over and chucked them out, all three of them, which I thought was a bit authoritarian of him. He did it very quietly and gently and thoughtfully, though, which is how he does everything. The Black kid looked as if he fancied making an issue of it, but she wouldn't let him. She had her hand on the nape of his neck, soothing him like that, while she talked very fast to Rupert, but quietly, so that I couldn't hear, and after a while Rupert started smiling too, a bit, but not all that much. Then they went. I was sure that as they went through the door she would turn round and smile at me, but she didn't.

After I'd finished my programme I went and had a shower. As I was dressing, Rupert came in. Rupert is so big that when he comes into a room it goes dark.

'All right, Alan?' Rupert makes a thing of knowing all the members' names, and treating us like friends. It's all business of course, but I can't help responding to it.

'Yeah, fine.' I had to ask him. 'What was the matter with those three you asked to leave then Rupert?'

'Ah them.'

'They were only laughing weren't they?'

'Not members, Alan. Just walked in off the street without a by your leave. I'm not insured for them for a start.' Rupert comes from Cumberland. He makes three indignant syllables out of the word 'insured'.

'Couldn't you have made them guests, or something?' He looked rather surprised at my saying that: I suppose I had never shown any interest in the running of the club before. 'I mean, they looked all right to me. Might have got three new members out of it.'

He shook his head, frowning.

'No. Trouble. They're not the sort of members I want, you see.'

'Why not?' I said.

He paused for quite a while, as if considering how to frame his answer. Eventually his face cleared.

'Well, I think they're criminals, you see.'

B

I hadn't been there in years. None of us had. I hadn't seen Damon and Mick for ages either, I'd been trying to keep out of all that. It was strange going down the gym again. The people were all different. Staring at us as if we were a bunch of wild animals. Made me want to laugh. Sometimes I think I *am* a wild animal.

The thing is I had been going stir crazy at the office for a while and I could feel one of my relapses coming on. And that morning I'd typed a letter off one of Desmond's audiotapes suggesting that Carol Rice might not be ideally suited to direct Stephen St John Coke's new screenplay, and Desmond and the rest of the guys had found that frightfully funny, Martin especially. I lost my temper and said well why can't the fucker spell his name properly like the rest of us, and that only made them laugh a lot more. They were sitting round in Desmond's office drinking a bottle of Sancerre and eating the sandwiches they'd sent me out for, and I found myself looking at Martin's blubbery lips and thinking I could just knock the top off the Sancerre and slice his top lip off and see how that went over with the assembled sophisticates.

Instead I walked out and went down the Albany where I knew I'd find Damon and Mick and they fell on my neck and we all wept a little and got slightly wrecked and then someone had the notion of crashing the gym, so we did. Simple as that.

A

When I was a little kid I used to like fairy stories and what I suppose you might call tales of chivalrous love. I liked Zorro and Captain Scarlet and all those as well of course and I can remember making my grandmother play Captain Scarlet with me in the woods – I had a sort of cloak thing and a zapper and I would crash through the bracken with the blood roaring in my head hearing my breath loud and harsh, enemies behind me, enemies ahead, the thick dark treetrunks looming at me one after another with Christ knows what blood-gorged bits of *spiritus mundi* lurking behind them, Captain Scarlet all alone Captain Scarlet far from home, has he at last gone too far, what terrible thing will heave itself up out of the shifting sands, bits of boy dangling nonchalantly from its slowly masticating jaws, and engulf him – but there were no girls in Captain Scarlet. I was particularly moved and intrigued by those episodes in *Star Trek*, and there were quite a few of them, when poor confused Kirk falls hopelessly in love with some alien girlchild whose belief systems and quite possibly organs of reproduction are wired up and programmed in some hopelessly Earth-unfriendly way. I think I understood at the time that they were absurd, these stories, but I also knew that they were true, for me.

Young boy goes in strange place.

My mother was, is, something of an authority on children's literature. It's her field. She writes it and she reads it and she writes about it and she is widely respected, as they all are, all those people who know what's good and bad for you better than you know it yourself. The sort of thing she writes is where the princess in the tower gets out herself and gets the giant working for her on an intermediate technology project involving wind and water power. Clever Gretchen, all that. Her stories are all right for her and for the little girl she never had but not for me.

There are other stories, stories that cut deeper, call to me from further down.

Stories of younger sons.

Young boy goes in strange place.

It is embarrassing to say this even to myself, but it is the truth: when I think about it, I realise that all my life I have been preparing myself to be the hero, to go in the strange place, to find the girl and save her and cherish her and be happy ever after.

B

B. Monkey.

Beatrice.

Being good now.

See me then though. On the cars, on the trains. Me and Bruno, we were magic.

B. Monkey. You've *seen* my name. But you can't read it because I always wrote it in my special way, and you have to look at it a bit before you can understand what it's saying, and most people don't know how to look. Ride the Metropolitan line one time, and open your fucking eyes for once. Squiggly writing on the inside yeah, squiggly writing on the outside. Squiggly writing on the walls as the tired old train clatters past and the shagged out citizens stare out with bleary eyes. Come on man, read the squiggly writing. B. Monkey, right? Royal Oak, Westbourne Park, Ladbroke Grove, Latimer, Goldhawk ... that was my fucking territory man! B. Monkey at the controls! Read my name!

There was a time when we could call on two hundred kids, we could have two hundred on the street, I only had to say the word, they were there. On the street. At my bidding. B. Monkey! Brilliant!

Don't ask me why.

Don't ask me why, I'll only say because.

Oh my only love my dear one I am scared to tell you all the things I have done in case they frighten or disgust you and you find you do not love me any more.

A

I had this little one-bedroom flat in Shepherds Bush then and the school was near the Lisson Grove estate. I would ride my bike to work. Fifteen, sixteen minutes. Best time, fourteen twenty. Captain Scarlet all alone, Captain Scarlet far from home. Push push push push. Good bike: I spent all the money I got for the car on it; people thought I was crazy.

I saw her as I was crossing Ladbroke Grove and at first I didn't realise it *was* her. Girl in a black suit creamy blouse high heels and bright red lipstick, very smart and flash, twenty-two or twenty-three years old, but striding and bouncing along swinging her bag like a kid with a satchel, so bright (I was passing her by now) and I thought hold on this is strange I've seen her somewhere – then I realised it was the same girl, the girl from the gym (I was only about five feet away from her for I suppose half a second) and she turned her head and looked straight into my eyes, and she started to laugh, and then I was past, and I turned my head to look and this time she turned back to look at me and she was still smiling.

But I was twenty yards up Blenheim Crescent by then and, as I saw when I turned my head, nearly into the back of a taxi, so that was that, except that all that day I found she got into all the chinks and notches, girl in the gym, girl in the suit, and was she laughing at me or for me, was she smiling because she liked the look of me or because she was a connoisseur of prats and dickheads? I do look a bit strange to some people, especially when I am on the bike. People have told me that I look like a mad beetle. Perhaps she just liked a laugh, and I was the funniest thing she had seen for a long time. I do have a little self-awareness. I do realise that the typical cyclist's physique, thin trunk and strong legs, is not especially attractive except to other cyclists, or beetles; likewise the typical cyclist's clothing. And my face is a bit of a problem too, it looks, I don't know, blunt, insensitive, *raw* somehow, it doesn't (if this doesn't sound absurd) look like *me*, and so often I have wished that I could rip my face off like a mask, tear it apart with my two hands so that the chosen one could look and see what a sensitive prince of man lurked underneath that manky carapace.

She got into the chinks and notches of the day. The mad kid in the gym, the suited office lady on her way to work.

And in the days that followed, I found she stayed with me. But only in the chinks and notches. The job I do, teaching very little kids, is fascinating and intricate, utterly absorbing from moment to moment. I wouldn't ever say I was obsessed with her, not then.

Not then.

Alan Furnace, twenty-six. Younger brother of Nick Furnace the 'prodigiously gifted' novelist. Younger son of Freddie Furnace, Professor Freddie Furnace that is, the . . . oh, I can't be bothered to list my dad's achievements, and Frances Furnace, née Fallow-field, under which name she still churns out her almost univer-sally applauded fictions for people under four feet tall. I was the quiet one. The shy one. The slow one. The dull one. The faintly disappointing one. Disappointing to them but honestly not really to myself; I think I was always marching to the beat of a different drum. (I came across that phrase when I was eleven and clung to it with deep devotion: it helped me to endure my adolescence, to survive the savage competitive strife that stood in for love in our family.)

Here is a typical example of the way I let the family down.

According to his own report, my brother Nick, en route to his First in Anthropology at Cambridge, fucked nearly all the famous beauties of his day, checking them off against one of his little lists. He told me so himself, perhaps intending it as a spur to similar achievements on my part. He was always being held up as an example to me, often by himself. (He is seven years older than I am, quite a gap. The ghost of a stillborn sister lies between us.)

I hate all that: competition, conquest, quantity. – Because you're a loser? whispers a little voice. Maybe. I honestly don't think I care. My talent, if it is a talent, seems to be for suffering and devotion, for love's longer distances. And the girls I fall for tend to be the wrong sort, except that for me they are right; my choices seem to embarrass other people. That's it.

So, having just scraped into UCL by the skin of my teeth, I fell deeply in love with one of the cleaners – Babbie, her name was. Irish. From Galway. She was seventeen years old, and I was eighteen. We were both lonely in London, and she was homesick too. We would stand kissing against the wall in a dark cobbled alley round the corner from the hostel, a couple of gauche waifs … she would talk continuously, just a series of stories about herself and her sisters – I think there were seven of them … their triumphs and misfortunes with the local boys, their complicated alliances and rivalries … she would talk too about the family dogs, one of whom, a greyhound called Gilhooley, she particularly missed and longed for and who, she said, was pining, off his food and crying for her at night, coming out of the trap slow and scanning the crowd for her, her father said. Her strict and loving father who would kill her, she said, if he knew what she was up to with me.

Venial sins and mortal sins. That was what she was up to with me. She was tormented by a complicated web of prohibitions and threats of purgatory and worse, but she loved me to stroke her large breasts, which I did with a kind of awe, and sometimes she would let me stroke her between her legs as well (the word *cunt* seems even now too coarse, too *urban* somehow for anything belonging to Babbie) but she loved that too, going into a kind of trance, sighing softly to herself, from time to time kissing me abstractedly with her soft gentle kisses … I was happy to go on for hours like this, marvelling at the mysterious intricacy I was exploring, the folding and unfolding and slackening and tightening, till eventually, sometimes, not always, her thighs would close tight and crush my fingers and she would stiffen, arch her back, and gasp, then sometimes shed tears.

Tears of joy, tears of remorse. She loved me too. She was too shy, I think, to take my prick in her hand and relieve me of my longing for her, and I was too shy, or something, to ask her. I think I was content with what I had: her closeness, her trust, her confidences, the comfort of her smell, the feel of her breath on my cheek, her arms around my neck . . . I would limp off to my lonely pit with savagely aching balls and fingers that looked as if I'd stayed in the bath too long, ecstatically happy. Feeling loved. She had strong square hands, bigger than mine, with broken fingernails. I loved them as much as anything about her. Her sweet rough hands.

I didn't want to go home for that first Christmas vac. She gave me an impractically large photograph of herself, A4 at least. It suited her in a way, she was a big girl, but I wanted one I could carry round with me, slip out of my wallet and study at the bus stop or in the slack moments of which there were plenty at the warehouse where I did my vac job, but I had to wait till I got home and I could sneak up to my room and let her slide out of my Stats file and look up at me: fair curly hair, huge blue eyes staring at the camera. And she wrote to me every other day, tender illiterate love letters with every other word misspelt. I didn't care, I didn't care, I loved her, she was my girlfriend, she was my own one.

My mother, who had never recognised any rights of privacy in others, and despite a full and busy life could always find time to poke around in other people's things, soon discovered both the photo and the letters. I had clearly done a very bad thing. First of all it was terminally naff of me to involve myself with a cleaner, and an Irish one at that, but this was not something that could be put like that, though that I am sure was her most powerful feeling. She also seemed able to feel simultaneously enraged as a woman, as a member of the sisterhood to which poor Babbie belonged as one of the weaker and more easily oppressed members, who was being used and abused by the young master. She took it for granted of course that we were shagging. My mother is a highly articulate woman. She had a great deal to say about Babbie and about me and about responsibility and power and exploitation and perversity and my father sat around and let her say it, though he had a shifty look on his face as he listened to her.

Then something very strange happened. Let me try to get this right. She was walking up and down, caught up in her own rhetoric, sounding as usual utterly convincing and being as usual utterly, destructively wrong, and I found myself for the first time trying to say this, trying in my dull and inarticulate way to tell her she had got it wrong and that this was something quite nice which was all mine and nothing to do with her, but I only got as far as saying something like 'Look you don't – ' and then I was not talking any more but involved in a desperate struggle to keep breathing and control the huge terrible sounds coming from deep down in my chest. She stopped shouting at me and started to stare at me in an amazed way as I fought with these mad loud noises that gradually transformed themselves into something quite ordinary, except that it was something I hadn't done since I was ten or eleven: I was sobbing noisily, first standing up, then on the sofa, throwing myself about and beating my face into the cushions, trying to speak but utterly failing, feeling totally misunderstood and buggered about. She simply stood and stared at me. I suppose she felt upstaged. I could see my father sitting gripping the arms of the chair. He looked . . . frightened. I was frightened myself. I didn't know how I was going to stop. Eventually she just walked out of the room, and after a few minutes I found I was able to get my breath and sit up. My father was looking at me in a worried way. After a while, he told me about this wine-tasting he was supposed to be looking in on, and asked me whether I'd like to go with him.

I couldn't think of any reason to say no.

On the way, he glanced at me several times; respectful is the way I would describe it. I seemed to have impressed him in some way. He seemed to feel that I was slightly dangerous. I found I rather enjoyed this. After a while he said something about it being a bit difficult for my mother at the moment. There was some sort of problem involving one of his research assistants; life, I was to understand, was complicated just now, even more complicated than it usually was. I said I wasn't interested. I said I just wanted to get on with my own life. He said he absolutely understood and appreciated that. Just before we went in, he said: 'You're not a bit like Nick, really, are you?

But then again, I don't think any of us are really, not even Nick if you see what I mean.'

Then we went in and started tasting the wine. There were a lot of men in dark business suits there; I think I looked a bit out of place in my jeans and tracksuit top and tearstains. I got talking to a man who told me his big secret: he had been in a major car accident and now had no sense of taste or smell at all. I asked him what he was doing at a wine-tasting in that case and he said he was getting ratarsed like everybody else.

I think that night was the only time I have felt even a little bit close to my fucking father.

Well, maybe when I was a baby. Maybe when I was a toddler. I have a half-buried memory, something to do with me in my Babygrow suit and him carrying me round and singing to me. Hey Mr Tambourine man play a song for Al. He used to call me Al. But that would be before he got disappointed with me.

A

When he sees her for the third time, in the stories, that is the time when he must make his move.

I saw her for the third time down the Institute. I used to go to a fencing class at the Institute. I loved it. The thing itself: the intricate steps, making patterns and breaking them, dominance and deviance, nature and culture, dancing and killing: as in boxing, you can't make it work unless you evolve a kind of dance with your partner and enemy, a shared pattern, and you can't win without breaking the pattern.

I wasn't much good at fencing because I loved making the pattern more than I loved disrupting it. I loved the way that every movement you can possibly make in fencing has been named and described centuries ago, and has its mirror image, its appropriate parry and riposte. Seen like this, the ideal bout would go on for ever, the partners perfectly matched. I wanted to do it right more than I wanted to win.

And it was so good, after a day of teaching little kids and getting them to behave like people, just to turn up and stop thinking and do what I was told. Our instructor had been a sergeant instructor in the Army, and he still liked to be called Sergeant Harris. All we had to do to please Sergeant Harris was to listen to what he said and carry out his instructions, to watch what he did and imitate it as exactly as we could. He had a dark red face and fierce blue bloodshot eyes. His hair and moustache were black and shiny, though he must have been well into his fifties: probably he dyed them. He wasn't vain, though – he seemed quite impervious to what anybody thought of him. Perhaps he regarded his hair and his moustache as part of his kit, along with his dazzling white T-shirt and his dazzling white canvas shoes, maintained to satisfy some private vision of swordsman's propriety.

Some of his pupils hated him for his calm rigidity. There was one goung guy, Graham, a student, who used to battle and irritate Sergeant Harris with his constant questions. 'But *why* do we have to do it like that?'
  'What?'
  'Why do we have to do it like *that*?'
  His serene incredulous glare.
'Why do we have to do it like that? We have to do it like that because I say so and because that is the right way to do it.'

Perfect.

I used to come out of Sergeant Harris's class feeling pure, focused . . . what's that word . . . shriven.

Yes.

So that when I saw her, B, B. Monkey, Beatrice, coming down the stairs, I wasn't even surprised. She didn't see me. Most of the classes finished around nine and there were a lot of people coming down the stairs, but she didn't seem to be with any of them. She looked different again, young again, like a kid, in her grey sweat top and a pair of jeans that looked as if they belonged to someone bigger. No make-up. She was wearing round spectacles and she was frowning to herself, and she looked as if she was muttering to herself as well – she looked like a little kid, like one of my little nutters, the way they stride about talking to themselves and frowning and scratching and dropping things. She was carrying a book, a paperback. I couldn't see what the title was.

I don't know why I didn't walk up to her and say something then, but I didn't. I wanted to watch her a little bit first.

She walked out of the Institute and turned left towards Holland Park Avenue. I walked behind her. The streetlamps were so sweetly spaced: just time to enjoy her as a silhouette, square-shouldered, bouncy, boyish, before she was under the light with her dark hair gleaming, then moving away, the light from that lamp clinging to her, sculpting her, then fading off her back until she started to belong to the next light, a silhouette again. I strolled behind her, with no idea of what I was going to do, but feeling in charge, feeling that I was looking after her, protecting her, even though I didn't even know her name.

I suppose we had walked past about six lamps when she turned. The lamp was midway between us.

'What d'you want?' she said. She sounded – not exactly frightened, but very tense, very tense and hostile. At first I was amazed that she should so misinterpret me, and then I thought, but of course, why wouldn't she? She didn't know she was destined to be my lover.
   'It's all right,' I said. 'I only wanted to talk to you.'
   'Just stay where you are,' she said.
   'I'm sorry,' I said. 'I didn't mean to frighten you.'
   'You don't,' she said. 'So fuck off now, all right?'
   She wasn't pleading with me. There was an element of threat in it, as if she held concealed some weapon I didn't know about, a gun or something, something she had used before and she could use again. On me. I felt it had all gone wrong. But I couldn't leave it. I couldn't turn away and leave her then. It was the third time and I had to make my move or it was all over for me. But I could think of only one word.
   'Please.'

I must have said it right.

   'Have I seen you before?' she said.
   'Yes! In the gym, you were with two boys, and then in the street, you were going to work, I was on my bike, I nearly hit a taxi looking back at you.'
   I must have started moving towards her because she said: 'No, don't come any closer, just stay there.' I started telling her who I was and where I worked. She interrupted me.
   'Look, what is all this, what do you want?'
   'I think I'm in love with you,' I said. It sounded an extremely stupid thing to say at fifteen paces. 'I want to go out with you.'
   She stared at me.

'You're mad, aren't you?'

'Not really. Bit eccentric.'

'No. Just stay there.'

She must have felt me wanting to move to her again. I stood still and so did she. It seemed to go on for quite a while. It was very interesting. Getting used to looking at each other. As we stood there I could feel her enmity fading, like a change of light or temperature.

'You think you're in *love* with me?'

'Yes.'

'But you don't know me.'

'Not yet.'

A long pause.

'No, this is stupid. You just want a fuck, don't you?'

I was shocked by her saying fuck: such a brutal word with all that space between us. But it was a serious question. I had to answer it truthfully. I thought for a bit.

'Not just.'

She laughed out loud, a brief little high bark, and then said, rather formally, I thought: 'Do you have a suggestion?'

I said we might go and have a drink.

'When?'

'Now?'

'I can't now,' she said. 'I got to go.'

'Tomorrow then?'

'Where?'

'D'you know Julie's?'

'Yeah. We talking about the wine bar or the restaurant?'

Shit, I thought. That's what you get for trying to impress.

I had to clear my throat.

'Um I thought the wine bar on the whole.'

'Cheaper, right?' she said, grinning.

'Well yes, but you know, nicer too. Less formal.'

'I bet you've never been there in your life,' she said.

She was right. Still, I soon would have, wouldn't I?

'Seven o'clock?'

'I haven't said I'll come yet.'

'I hope you will.'

'Yeah, being in love with me and everything.'

I waited.

'Be there at seven,' she said. 'Inside. Upstairs. You might see me, you might not. If I do come, I won't be late. OK?'

'Yes,' I said. 'Thank you.'

'Thank you for asking me. My name is Beatrice,' she said. 'I'm going now. Goodnight.'

She turned and walked off. I understood that I was not to follow her.

B

He thinks I am extraordinary but I'm not, not really, I've just had rather a strange life, and I suppose I've had my moments. But the wriggly writing is faded now and you can hardly read my name at all.

He's odder than me, really.

Ah, who gives a fuck? We're all a bit fucking strange aren't we, but I dare say we all feel perfectly normal inside.

The book I had that night was *Crime and Punishment*.

It started when I went to secondary school. I didn't like the teachers and I didn't like the other girls. The teachers at the primary school thought I was nice and funny and quite clever in my monkeyish style and I never gave them any grief nor they me. Mrs Marsden and Miss Harris and them, they were gentle with us and they liked a laugh and I think they thought I was a very nice girl. No one made a big deal about the free dinners. Lots of the kids were on free dinners at that school. Nobody minded much about what anybody else was wearing. I was dressed mostly out of jumble sales but my mum was a good chooser and I too knew what I looked good in, even when I was little. And if I longed for something new expensive and my own, it was a private longing. No one mocked me or gave me a hard time about being poor or having funny clothes or having a funny name.

Beatrice.

Beatrice Robson, actually.

It's not a funny name, it's an Italian name. My mother is Italian. She chose my name. Say it in English, it sounds like a fucking root vegetable or something, say it in Italian it sounds magnificent: Bay Ah Tree Chay, Bay Ah Tree Chay, Bay Ah Tree Chay! Like a cry of desperate passion!

Beetriss Robson, though. Bit creepy. Sounds like the sadistic matron of some murky old folks' home. Police today were interviewing Beetriss Robson following the deaths in mysterious circumstances of seventeen of her elderly charges. Q: How do you poison an old lady with a razorblade? A: Give her arsenic.

Beatrice. Not a pretty name.

Except when he says it. My dear one, my young husband. Beatrice. He says it the English way, but he makes it sound so tender, like undoing buttons.

B. Monkey though.

Saying that still makes me want to get up and dance.

Oh but I saw him burning I saw him burning.

It was an accident an accident

I saw him burning

Talk about something else oh yes that fucking secondary school full of rich nasty bastards and suddenly everything about me was wrong my shoes my jeans I was only eleven years old and at the mercy of the fucking style police. On my first day I turned up in my monkey boots. Remember monkey boots, like Docs for midgets? In my junior school they thought my monkey boots were fine; in the secondary school there was a bunch of girls who wanted to beat me up for wearing them. Monkey boots, monkey boots, Robson's a monkey wearing monkey boots. I didn't know how to fight or anything then, good job I could run.

But that's not what a liberal education is supposed to be about though is it eh? Someone high up should look into it that is my opinion.

The teachers too were not interested in what I had to say, only in getting me to say what they wanted to hear. So I stopped talking to them. I pretended to be a retard. I cultivated a moronic grin, all slitty-eyed and wrinkling my nose up. They bought it. Thus did I preserve the integrity of my private soul. My subhuman leer disturbed them; they used to let me lurk off to the bogs for hours on end ... Jesus, that was boring. Smelly, too. And the company was depressing; most of my fellow bog-lurkers really were moronic. Outcasts and victims: Darlene Styles, Jenny Quick, Alma Koon. I was the brains of that little outfit, the brains and the beauty too, they all admired me, they wanted to touch me all the time, to put my hair in little plaits, but I shied away from it, and it was not just Jenny's smelly knickers and Darlene's impetigo, it was I suppose their terrible neediness and all one way, they didn't understand that I was needy too. And it was such a scary feeling, that the floor had rotted under my feet and I had fallen through and here I was for ever doomed to live in a subterranean toilet with these smelly pubertal juvenile well *bag ladies* really ...

I started having days off, then weeks. My mum was OK. She wrote me notes when I asked her to, she knew what it was like, not wanting to go out and face the day, her day being stacking shelves and cleaning other people's houses. I understood that my father going off the way he did, no note, no explanation, it had somehow robbed her of her will, her I don't know her energy her *desire* not just sexual her urge to make a mark on life you know like Read My Name You Fuckers all that stuff ... but it didn't stop her being nice to me but in a gentle resigned sort of way that made me want to howl out loud, tickle her till she screamed with laughter, burn the fucking house down ...

No, not that.

I was only three when my dad went off.

She never wanted anyone else.

Well a few times she did bring blokes back. Just a few times. I could always hear them. I could always hear everything though I tried not to. They weren't all horrible, one or two of them sounded quite kind and gentle with it. Two or three of them stayed all night. None of them came back a second time.

Once when I went to the supermarket where she stacked the shelves in the evening, I was a bit early, they were having a laugh, the blokes, they were all singing this song that was supposed to be Italian with lines in it like What's A Matter You and Shut Uppa Your Face and my mum was supposed to be laughing along with them being a good sport all that, and she was doing her best, but you could see she didn't like it very much, or not at all really. I hate that 'what's the matter ain't you got no sense of humour love' stuff.

I went back a few years later to have a look round the supermarket, see if any of them were still working there. Most of them had left, but one of them, Dick his name was (and his nature ha ha), he was still there. He seemed to have progressed from fruit and veg to under-manager. Meteoric rise to fame. He didn't recognise me at all. I watched to see which one his car was: an old Capri but with all the trimmings, leopardskin seats mag wheels a ten foot aerial the lot. It was parked over the road from the shop – just right. I waited till it was getting dark and then I whacked the boot lock (old spark plug and hammer, the Capri was ever a doddle) took out the dickhead's own spare can of fuel, poured it liberally as indicated, and set his car on fire.

Don't believe that bollocks in the films where they have to run for their lives and fling themselves headlong up each other's arses before a mighty explosion rocks the universe: any car I've torched, I've had plenty of time to stroll away to a place of safety before the tank blows. As on this occasion, I was able to mingle innocently with the little band of fascinated spectators as my enemy came running out of the shop dancing about and yelling in a most satisfactory way. I did think of strolling over and asking him what the matter was and had he temporarily lost his well-known sense of humour, but I judged that to be rash.

30

I think I must already have been starting to settle down.

Yes, stupid really. And of course he would claim on his insurance, but you could tell the dickhead really loved that stupid car. I cannot really make myself regret it, not really.

I used to adore a bit of arson.

But I saw him burning

A

The sun is obscured by cloud and it is very low in the sky which is a harsh metallic dirty colour, hard on the eyes. The hedges are very black. The grass is ankle high, tussocky, grey, exhausted-looking. There are thirty or forty of us walking steadily across the big field. All men. I am the youngest of the men. I am walking with them, but I don't feel as if I belong with them. They look like serious men: heavy set, wearing old tweed jackets in subdued greys and greens, droplets of dew gleaming in the fibres. Their boots are heavy. They all carry sticks. The sticks are something more than walking sticks: they are the kind of sticks that you could break a man's back with. I have a stick too. It is heavy; the weight of it is tiring my wrist as I walk. Nobody speaks. The only sounds are the boots swishing through the grass and the steady breathing of the men.

There is a path across the field, but there are too many of us for the path; we are spread out on either side of it. The field slopes upwards, falling gently away to either side, and it is so large that the black boundary hedge forms the horizon. A child might imagine that we were walking towards the edge of the world.

I feel as if we are marching towards the edge of the world. And I am worried about who I am with and why we are there.

I look at the man on my right and the man on my left. Their faces are closed and intent. They do not want to be spoken to. I begin to realise that they are going to do something so terrible that they cannot speak of it. If they spoke of it, it would render them incapable of doing it.

I realise too that my presence makes them feel uncomfortable. But they are not going to let that stop them.

We are getting near the hedge at the edge of the world now. At the highest point there is an ordinary five-barred gate. The first man has reached it, and he is holding it open for the rest of us.

As the men shuffle together to go through the gate I can hear a low murmur. I cannot make the words out, but now I understand what these men are here for. They are going to do something to Beatrice. With their sticks. There is something terrible that they have to do, and I understand that there is no use arguing with them. They have no more choice in this matter than their sticks have.

I have a choice, of course. I can join them, which is unthinkable. I can watch what they do. I can try to run away. I can try to defend her, one against forty. Perhaps she will be able to run away while they are killing me.

I go through the gate into the field on the other side, and as soon as I have gone through I realise with huge relief that she is not there any more; she has got away, she has outwitted them. The field is empty.

I turn to face the men. The sun comes out. I can feel it warm on my face.

I was early at Julie's of course. All dressed up, or as dressed up as I could be: I had a black tweed jacket that was not too bad and a black polo shirt and Levis. I went inside and upstairs. No one stopped me though a couple of them looked as if they might be thinking of it, or perhaps that was just my imagination.

There was no one at the bar, just a few people sitting at little tables. I went to the bar. The woman behind it looked at me a little warily I thought as if I was a holdup man or something. I asked her if I could have a glass of wine.
  'Yes, sure,' she said. 'Why don't you sit down and I'll bring you a list?'

I went and sat down in the corner. Almost as soon as I got there I thought of what I should have said: 'No, why don't I just stand here while you pour me a glass of fucking wine like I fucking asked you to?' *Esprit d'escalier*, I believe that's called. Actually I have never spoken to anyone like that in my life except possibly my brother, and he used to beat me up for it ... A couple of smart-looking women at one of the tables were looking at me and one of them said something to the other and the other one smiled. I felt myself starting to blush. This was a disaster. Why hadn't I asked her to meet me in a pub or just on a corner or something? Because I wanted to make it special, that's why. I thought of going downstairs and hanging about outside and taking her somewhere else when she turned up, if she turned up. No, she might not like that. Inside, she had said. Inside. Upstairs. Oh shit.

After what seemed like about twenty minutes the waitress decided I had been punished enough and strolled over with the list. I ordered a glass of house Côtes du Rhône – no cackles of laughter or snorts of derision, no incredulous glances from the other clients – and I started to feel a lot better. It was all right, this place. I could handle it. I'm generally OK on my own. I keep still, I breathe steadily, I let my eyes go out of focus. I let the thoughts drift in and out of my head, or I pick something to think about, or I watch other people and listen to them. I don't need a book or a paper. In the months before I met her, I had been spending nearly all my free time alone. I was in practice.

I was able to hear fragments of several conversations. One of the smart-looking women was telling the other one how she had that morning lost her job because some bastard called Richard had declared her to be redundant while practically in the same breath informing the directors that he couldn't possibly cope unless he had a new secretary so that this *hopeless* and *ignorant* but wouldn't you know it breathtakingly arrogant *assistant* who of *course* he was *fucking* and had been for *months* could step into a *newly created post* whose job description sounded more or less *identical to the one she'd just been made redundant from.*
    'Tribunal, darling. Sue him to pieces. *I* would.'
    'You must be joking. This is the music business. I'd never work again.'

The woman who had been made redundant started to cry. The other woman took tissues from her bag and handed them to her friend one by one. The one who was not crying looked sharply over in my direction. I looked past her. A woman came up the stairs and my heart gave a thump but she was not Beatrice.

On the table behind me a man and a woman were talking. They seemed to be meeting for the first time. The woman was doing most of the talking: she was telling the man about the breakup of her marriage. She was telling him that she had had her problems but she thought she was over them now; however she needed very sensitive handling. She liked nice things and was artistic in temperament: she was an antiquey sort of person, she said. She was telling this man whose face I could not see that she would be very frank with him; he had a sensitive face and she was sure he would understand. She had a tendency to harm herself and had been sectioned twice because of this. (Sectioned? An image flashed into my mind of some sort of medieval punishment, like quartering.) Then I heard a chair scrape and the woman asking the man why he as getting up. He said he was sorry but there had been a failure of communication. He had specified that he was only interested in slim ladies under forty. He walked past my table on his way to the stairs, but I could not see his face.

As he walked down the stairs he almost bumped into another woman who was not Beatrice. As this woman reached the top of the stairs she looked over towards me. She was about thirty. She had a thin anxious face. She looked anxiously around the room and then her gaze came to rest on me. I felt anxious. For a few moments nothing else happened: she looked anxiously at me and I looked anxiously at her. Then she came hesitantly towards me. I realised that she must be a friend or a colleague of Beatrice's and she had come to tell me that Beatrice would be late, or that she couldn't come that night, or most likely that she had decided she didn't want to see me at all, and resigned myself to despair.

The woman asked me if my name was Bernard. I said that it wasn't, and she went off and sat in the corner by herself. She had a very pale face and reddish hair. She kept looking at her watch, and once she shook it and held it to her ear to see if it was going.

Behind me, the woman who had been sectioned twice, whose face I still had not seen, began to cry softly.

I looked around the bar. It was beginning to fill up with tense unhappy-looking couples. I caught some more fragments of conversation. People were asking each other extraordinary impossible things, such as what kind of music they liked and whether they had any hobbies and whether they preferred the town or the country. I had a brief spell of sick panic when I thought that Julie's could not be a wine bar at all: it was a front for some clandestine criminal activity – as soon as I had gone these people would talk about the real purposes of their meeting – credit card fraud, industrial espionage, ritual child murder . . . Or perhaps it was just some sort of language school where the students were practising their idiomatic English in pairs: if so, their teacher had worked hard on their accents, but their vocabulary and syntax were hopelessly stilted. Then a tall man with a haunted face and only one ear came up the stairs and stood looking anxiously around the room before walking hesitantly towards the woman with reddish hair. She greeted him with what looked like a mixture of relief and dismay. He must, I realised, be Bernard.

And Julie's, I realised, must be recommended by some fucking computer dating agency as an ideal place for that crucial first date. Oh fuck. Oh fuck fuck fuck fuck fuck fuck fuck fuck *fuck*.

Suddenly a woman walked very quickly up the stairs and strode directly to my table with her head down, and this time it was Beatrice.

You sat down without looking at me, and stared down at the table. All I could see was the top of your head. Your dark brown hair looked very shiny and clean. You were wearing the black office-lady suit I had seen you wearing in the street, and a creamy-coloured blouse, open at the throat in a deep V. I felt that there was more to see down there than I had a right to see just then . . . is that stupid? Well, I felt that. Your arms were on the table. They looked very tense. Neither of us had said anything. I felt so strange. My ears were buzzing.

Then you looked up at me, and I saw your bright brown eyes close to for the first time, and I felt as if no one had ever really looked at me before. I knew that you were seeing me. *Seeing* me. Seeing *me*. I heard myself make this really stupid high little sound, the sort of sound that dogs make when they are trying to speak, and you smiled, and I suppose I was smiling back, and you went on smiling . . . I was astonished because every time I had seen you you had seemed so utterly self-confident and sort of centred, but this was such a . . . *needy* smile. And I understood a whole lot of things at once, they all came flooding in: she's like me, I thought, she puts her whole self in, she can't help it, whatever it is, she goes all the way, and that's why she's scared, it's not me she's scared of, it's herself. And I knew that whatever happened it was going to be OK. I knew that absolutely and with blinding confidence, and I told you.

'It's OK.' I said. 'It's OK. Really. It's OK.'
  'What's OK?' you said.
  'Everything,' I said. 'I guarantee it. It's going to be wonderful. It's going to be OK.'

Your smile was enormous. You looked about four years old. I noticed for the first time your sweet flat nose and your large irregular nostrils, and I thought some people would think that was ugly, but I know she's beautiful, only I know how beautiful she is.
  'It's OK,' I told her. 'It's OK.'

I can't remember much about what we said that first night, although we talked for three hours and somehow got through three bottles of wine. She was happy to be with me and it was all OK. The doomed daters came and went, the waitress wafted about and actually came to seem quite benevolent after a while, and we sat and looked at each other and talked and talked and looked. It was the looking more than the talking.

I knew that she could see me.

The prince of men beneath the manky carapace.

I knew that she could see how I could love her.

One thing I remember, something so extraordinary that the next day I wondered if I had dreamed it.

We had been talking, and fallen silent. We both had our hands on the table. I think I had half-consciously been waiting for a signal that it was time to take her hand in mine. Then, to my astonishment, she took my hand in hers and drew it to her, slipped it inside her blouse and over her bare breast. It felt soft and warm, fuller than I had expected. I could hardly breathe.

'Can you feel it?' she said.
  'Your breast?' I said, stupidly.
  'My heart,' she said.

B

Not bad for the first date, what d'you reckon?

Bit what, bit forward?

I couldn't wait for him to touch me. My heart was beating so fast. I would have liked to take his hand and thrust it under my skirt, and see his eyes go wide with amazement as he felt how wet I was, and then I would say, 'That's for you.' I think that would have been a nice thing to do, but I wasn't sure what he would think about it; he might just think I was a dirty slut. It was, after all, I had to remind myself, a very early stage in our relationship.

His hands were soft and gentle, quite big. Bigger than Paul's. I was with Paul at that time. You try not to compare but you can't help it really. Of course we're all unique and every relationship is utterly unlike every other and nothing compares with nothing, but some people are gentle and some are rough and impatient, and some people have big hands and some people have small ones. Etcetera.

I am sure he thought, thinks, that was the first time I'd ever done that, taken someone's hand and put it inside my dress to feel my heart.

I wish it was.

We drank three bottles of wine. At that time I could drink three bottles on my own and walk out with my head held high. He was well away that night, Alan, though he had no idea he was.

He thought it was all the power of love I expect, and it was that too, it was, it wasn't just the wine.

I thought it was going to be difficult, talking, I mean, that night, but it was easy. It was easy because he did just about all the talking. He talked a lot about himself and teaching little kids, and how his parents despised him for doing that and how he didn't give a fuck though you could see he did really. He has a bit of a problem with his parents and so would I have, I think, if I had his parents. I thought it's funny, you have problems and I *am* a problem. He talked quite a bit about the kids he teaches and he sounded nice when he was doing that and I thought I would not have minded having this guy for my teacher when I was a little girl. Or even when I was a big girl ha ha. And I was already thinking there were one or two things I knew I would not mind teaching him.

When he'd finished telling me about himself he started telling me about me. He wanted to tell me he thought I was beautiful, and that was very nice, in fact it was lovely, but I could see he thought he was the only one in the world who was capable of perceiving my loveliness. It never seemed to cross his mind that other people might have been turned on to the point of gibbering madness by my face and my body.

That didn't matter, I didn't give a fuck if you want to know the truth, because there was something about him I had seen in the street and was still there in the bar, something I'd been missing, wanting, something, *extreme*, something *all the way*, something *deep friends* something *die for each other*, like Paul was out on a limb in his lazy way, but this one was in a whole different gear, he wanted to go all the way, you could see it in his eyes, the set of his body, I wasn't really listening to what he was saying, I was just like *smelling him out*, and what I was smelling was that here was a boy I could oh fuck what is that word something like a fence oh that's it *impale* myself on. Yeah!

Been sending out my signal on my special frequency and it hovers in the hot black night, it hovers unique on the airwaves, my unique cunt fragrance carried on the breeze, it's not for you, not for you, not for you, but for him, my unique one, my dear one, my stranger, and he comes now, out of the night he comes and does not fail, it sounds like crap but I believe it, I fucking do, and anyone who hasn't felt it I fucking well feel sorry for them.

I have to admit though he was a bit funny about spending money. He seemed amazed when I hailed a cab. (There was a nice BMW outside Julie's I could have been into in twelve and a half seconds but I didn't want to give him too many surprises in one evening. And anyway I'd made a vow to give it up, the cars, all that.

Since Bruno.)

Kissing in the taxi he held my face between his hands. He didn't know he could have done anything he liked with me.

He didn't seem to think it was strange, a bit of rough like me living on Prince of Wales Drive. Though no doubt he didn't see me as a bit of rough. Perhaps by then I already wasn't. I'd been working for the company for quite a while, learning something every day, even if it's only how Karel Reisz spells his name, and I was no stranger to restaurants and taxis. And Paul I suppose was a bit of a sophisticate in his clapped-out seventies style . . . we were leaning up against a lamppost kissing and at the same time I was trying to squint up to the flat to see if he was in, Paul that is. He was supposed to be in Ibiza but he was always reappearing. Always turning up when he was supposed to be in Ibiza, always fucking off to Morocco or somewhere when he was supposed to be here. A desperately, an extravagantly unreliable man. I knew that he wouldn't mind my asking Alan up, but I thought that it would freak Alan out to meet my degenerate old lover on his first night with me. I didn't want to screw up. I think I knew even then that Paul was receding into the past and Alan was the future. I didn't want to scare him off.

But the flat was dark and I decided to take a chance on it and asked him if he'd like to come up. And he said no. I said making a joke what's the matter don't you do it on the first date, and he said no, he didn't want to spoil things by rushing them; he said that meeting me had been very important for him and he wanted to get everything right. I felt chastened. It was as if he'd said I

43

was trying to spoil things by rushing them. I think he could see what I was feeling because he said he was sorry and he was a dickhead and of course he would love to come up; but I said no, if that was how he felt he was probably right and we should say goodnight – I ask you what a load of Jane Austen bollocks, that was nearly it, there and then, I was that close, it was on the tip of my tongue to say all right fuck off for ever darling I cannot be doing with one second more of this Jane Austen bollocks – but then he took my face in his hands again (his one trick but a good one) and he said:

'It's OK. Really. It's OK.'
   And I said: 'What's OK?'
   And he said: 'Everything is. Really. It's going to be OK.'

And it was, really.

Until the past started bleeding into the future.

Paul wasn't there.

The flat felt dark and hot and full of dust and ash and unfinished business. I went in the bathroom and had a shower and that felt good; my body felt strong and slippery in the steam. Then I went and lay down on the bed and played with myself, imagining my new young lover running home across the Albert Bridge, his quick breath, bright eyes, over the dark glittering river, and then we were back in the wine bar, and he was falling in love with me, yearning for me across the table, and then I took his hand and held it to my breast, and he gasped, and then I took his hand and slipped it under my skirt so that he could feel my cunt all warm and wet for him, and then we both slipped down under the table and I could see people's legs, the girls that worked there walking past, and someone saying 'Is this table taken?' and we were trying to wriggle out of our clothes so that he could get inside me, but something was in the way and I was wide open reaching for him but he was stuck, jammed somehow, with his head pressing hard into my neck forcing my chin back and I pushed against his face and saw that it wasn't him at all any more, it was Bruno it was Bruno his pale crazy eyes, it

44

was poor Bruno, and I shut my eyes tight and tried to block him out and bring Alan back but it was no good, I had lost it.

I lay in the hot dusty darkness listening to the little late night creakings inside the flat and the car outside. The muffled hooting of the river barges as they beat their way upstream against the current. I imagined the rats scrabbling in the bilges, the way they do in the stories.

I thought, I have got to get out of this.

A

What kind of music do you like?

Do you have any hobbies?

Which do you prefer, the country or the town?

I like any kind of music that hits the spot. Brahms. Basie. Billie Holliday.

Yes, I have hobbies.

On the whole I prefer the country to the town, but now I think that if they want to hurt you badly enough they will come after you and find you anywhere.

When I was about six I went through this phase of being obsessed with war. War, guns, bombs, shooting, killing, army, fighting, blood. I read about it in the comics and I watched it on TV. Men in steel helmets lying in the gutter or pressed into doorways, anxiously covering each other, while women would hurry past with babies in prams and little kids like me would go past on their way to school. Villages of straw huts on fire and people running out of them. Some of the people were burning. They were the enemy.

I used to draw a lot of pictures about war. Bombers would fly through the sky dropping their bombs and the tanks and planes would fire at them. Sometimes bits of people would fly through the air, heads, arms and legs, with blood coming out of the stumps. These were people like you and me who had not been able to take shelter or get in one of the tanks. If you were in one of the tanks you were safe.

I began to specialise in tanks. At first the tanks were quite small, with just one man in a steel helmet operating the anti-aircraft gun, while the bombs rained down around him. But gradually my tanks evolved so that they could accommodate more and more people: families of people, and eventually streets of people. You could see their faces peering out through the long narrow windows that ran all down the sides of my tanks. They were smiling. They were smiling because they were safe in the tanks. In the end my tanks got so big that they filled the entire picture space and there was no room for the planes and the bombs. The people were squashed up very tight in the tanks, but there was room for them all.

I had saved all the people.

But I had to fill a whole wall with these drawings before I was satisfied with my work.

I couldn't believe my ears.

'But what did you *do*?' I said.
  'Most things really,' she said.
  'But like that?'
  'Like street robbery. And robbing cars, and robbing from cars, and t.d.a. And theft, and burglary, a bit, and just sort of general messing about and fighting. Affray, they call that. Good word, eh?'
  'Wonderful,' I said.
  'Armed robbery,' she said.
  'Oh, come *on*,' I said.
  'Better believe it, read my name,' she said.
  'So, um you must have done quite a bit of time,' I said.
  'Never been inside that place, not once, man.'
  She was grinning.

'Bribed the police, I expect.'
'Nah, we just used to intimidate the witnesses.'

We were in Julie's again. She was eating the sausage and mash.

'Arson,' she said. 'Extortion.'
   'Any murders at all?'
   'Well,' she said. 'Not exactly. I mean . . . not technically.'
   'You're winding me up, aren't you?' I said.
   She smiled.
   'If you like.'
   'You are. Aren't you?'
   'If you like.'
   'I fucking well hope you are.'
   "Well, I am then,' she said.

She ate some more sausage and then she put her fork down and took my hand.

'Don't be frightened, Alan,' she said. 'It's only me.'

B

But I think he was.

You'd think he could see he could do what he liked with me.

But I think he was.

I think he was frightened of me.

A

The trouble was . . .

No.

Oh, come on, don't be so pathetic. Come on, Prince. Let's have you. *Talk* about it. You're only talking to yourself, after all.

When I was fourteen or fifteen I used to walk home from school sometimes with a boy called Jimmy Dwyer: he was a Roman Catholic and went to a Roman Catholic school. He was really into all that Catholic doctrine, and he got me interested too. He had all these little posers that sounded like riddles but were in fact ethical and religious problems, such as : If you were alone on a desert island without any other people or even animals, which sin might you be prey to? I suggested gluttony, blasphemy and despair, but it turned out that the sin he had in mind was self-abuse.

What made me think of that now? Oh, yes. If you were alone on a desert island, which in a sense is where we all are, a lot of the time, is it possible to conceive of the state of embarrassment? Is it not the most social of all sensations? Wouldn't it be impossible to be embarrassed when there's no one about to witness one's shame? Isn't embarrassment essentially *about* someone else seeing you in a shameful situation?

Of course it is.

And what's shameful about it, anyway?

Nothing. Nothing at all.

So why can't I . . .?

I don't know. I just can't. I'll just have to leave all that bit out.

B

We couldn't get it on! We couldn't do it! We couldn't get it in!

The first time we tried was in Paul's place. I knew for certain this time that Paul was not going to be there because he had phoned me that afternoon from Sydney with a message to pass on. He had been in Australia for a week and he hadn't even told me he was going to be out of London. (What's happening, he kept saying, what's happening, how are you, how are you feeling, I'm worried about you, I don't feel right without you, we need to talk, we ought to be together more Benny . . . He liked to call me Benny, I'm not sure why, I asked him once and he said because I gave him such a rush but maybe he liked to think of me a bit like a boy. Benny, I wish you were with me, the ferries in the harbour look like little bath toys, Benny I've been thinking we can get our life right soon as I get back . . . He always went on like that, Paul, it never meant anything much, it was just like scratching his arse to him. Old Paul. And I had been so excited the first time he touched me. Different person then. And I thought again, I have got to get out of this and give myself a chance you are such a loser Paul you and your exhausted expertise your skilful fingers reaching up out of the swamp to drag me down again and again . . . get out of this, get out of this, I thought.)

I asked him, Alan, if he would like to come up this time, and I knew he would say yes, and he did. We both knew what it was all about. I was as scared as he was; I think he infected me with this intensity he had. I looked at his face as we came into the hall downstairs, and it was all white, and his lips looked dark, and when I took his hand I could feel him trembling even though he was warm, and then I started trembling too. My legs felt weak and I wondered how we were going to get up all the stairs. There were seven flights of them, wide shallow steps covered with thick carpet, that colour they call old gold. Quite . . . grand, really, they were, in a faded sort of way, very Paulish, he liked to tell people he lived in 'what a social climber would call a mansion block' as if he wasn't one himself, social fucking chimpanzee, him. Anyway, there were all these stairs, and I could see them daunting Alan more than somewhat. We trudged up, Alan and I, hand in hand, and it seemed that neither of us could think of anything to say. All that long lonely climb. Each step I took I could feel the inside of my head getting colder.

Big heavy door. It always groaned as you pushed it open.

As soon as we were inside I knew it was a mistake to bring him here for our first time. With Alan beside me holding my hand I realised how strong that flat smelt of Paul. Not just his dogends and his aftershave, but *him*, the air seemed to be full of him, I thought I could smell whiffs of his skin, his sweat, his spunk, even his shit. I thought, that's impossible, what's making me think these thoughts, but they wouldn't go away.

Alan was looking around in a baffled sort of way. 'You like lamps,' he said. He was staring at the lamps. Paul has about three hundred of them squatting around waiting to come back into fashion or something: semi-naked ladies, fish, dogs, cats, birds, ballerinas . . . I believe some star he was fucking once told Paul a man should have a hobby and suggested that he start collecting lamps. Paul always follows the advice of famous people. I think he is hoping that these lamps will give shape and meaning to his life. He keeps forgetting that he already has something that gives shape and meaning to his life.

'It's all right,' I told Alan. 'I don't like the lamps. They're not my lamps. It's not my flat. I just look after it for the guy who owns it. He lets me live here, you know?' I sounded shifty even to myself. And Paul's smells seemed to be getting stronger all the time.

Now Alan was looking at the piano.
 'He's a musician, is he?'
 'No,' I said. 'He just has this piano.'

I tried to explain about the piano, about how Paul believed that in this life you had to have the grand piano with the photographs, that if you didn't have the grand piano with the photographs you were fucked. And that the photographs had to be *framed* and *signed* and at least half of them had to be of famous people, and at least half of them had to have Paul in the photograph as well, touching the famous person or being touched by them, smiling proudly out at the camera, saying see me touching these rich and famous people, and the famous people smiling tolerantly out at the camera, saying yes, we know Paul, we let him touch us, we are not afraid of catching his diseases . . . Paul doesn't like to tell lies, he's sort of superstitious about lying. So he never exactly says that these rich and famous people are old and dear friends of his, that they are people he has worked with and is working with or is shortly to be working with on a major movie project. He just allows you to infer it.

Infer. Imply. You make an implication. I draw an inference from it. Take an evening class and change your life . . .

The truth is of course that the people in the photographs don't really want to be friends with Paul or have him direct movies for them. They just want Paul to get drugs for them.

I judged it best not to tell Alan about the drugs.

But I did tell him some stuff about Paul. More than I meant to, too much really, but I didn't seem to be able to stop, and Paul's smell getting stronger and stronger . . . I was rubbing my finger in the dust on the piano, making a sort of star pattern, and then I saw that he was doing the same thing, rubbing *his* finger in the dust, in this embarrassed miserable well desolate way really, and I understood that he was thinking 'she fucks with this Paul' and I wished he would ask me if I did so that I could say 'yes but not any more now, it's you, it's you' but he didn't so I couldn't. Oh dear oh dear life is complicated. I thought we might dive into bed as easy as dive into a pool, and . . . shag like angels, and here we were standing rubbing dust about on Paul's fucking piano. Hopeless, hopeless. I sort of ground to a halt and managed to look up at him and give him a little smile, and he smiled back, after a fashion. He gave a sort of wincing grimace.

'It's OK,' he said, and his voice was all trembly. 'It's really OK, it's fine.'

We were like a couple of people waiting to go into the room where they cut your legs off.

I took hold of his hand and I think I said 'come on then'. We walked into the bedroom: it was always too warm in there, hot and thick and dusty, always a relief to get your clothes off, and I took mine off then, quickly, facing him, smiling – he was just standing there watching me – and I started to feel excited. I was standing there in just my socks and he hadn't taken anything off, he hadn't moved. I said, 'Come on, you're cheating' and he still didn't move. I did my well-known party trick, standing on my left leg and lifting my right leg up high to pull my sock off without bending, and he gave a little gasp, and I thought this is more like it. I went and put my arms round him and let him feel me against him: I was so excited that I thought it could be quite nice if he just pushed me over and gave me one, just like that, without stopping to take his clothes off, a brisk rousing overture before the main programme sort of thing; but I could feel he was too tense for that and I suppose more to the point he didn't seem to be hard yet. I kissed him and it felt as if his mind was somewhere else and I started to think 'he doesn't like me, he doesn't like me, he thought he was in love with me but now he knows me he thinks I'm just a slag and he can't find any way of saying it' and then I started to feel awful and not excited any more, so I let go of him and just sort of slipped into bed and hoped for the best.

And then he took his clothes off and I watched him out of the corner of my eye while he was doing it. He looked so miserable and tense. His body was pale, thin but strong, with big legs. I got a flash of his pubic hair, a big bright black bush of it, and his soft thick cock, a lovely body really I thought, why don't I want him and why doesn't he want me, and then I actually started feeling a bit sick, well more than a bit really, just nerves and

58

misery, no doubt, and the thought flashed across my mind, how dreadful if I puke on him while we're actually doing it . . . little did I know how awful it was really going to be.

The sex lives of young people today.

We snuggled together but he felt tense and cold and all sharp corners. Somehow we didn't seem to be able to make ourselves comfortable against each other. He started to kiss me in an anxious bruising sort of way, not a bit like the sweet soft kisses we'd had before, I wanted to melt him down but his face felt all stiff and when I put my arms round him his shoulders were tense and straining and I thought oh, Alan, everything about you's stiff except the bit that ought to be. 'You're so lovely' he said, in a grinding irritable tone. 'Your eyes . . . they're such a wonderful bright brown.'

There we were, both trying desperately to get into the mood, thoughts flying everywhere, both of us saying the wrong thing . . . I actually wanted to say all very well the bright brown eyes, but we've had all that, is something the matter with the tits or what, what is it, what have I done wrong, why don't you fancy me, why are you making me feel like a slag, and then I did hear myself asking him in this little timid voice what the matter was, and he said: 'Nothing. It's fine. It's OK. Everything is going to be OK. I'm just a bit in awe of you that's all.'

In awe? Of me?

So we started trying properly, but it was hopeless. We started off cold and tense but it wasn't any better when we were hot and sweaty, nothing seemed to work, he kept trying to put it inside me when he was only half hard, muttering about how it was OK, OK, everything was going to be OK, when it was obvious it wasn't OK at all. And the bed got hotter and hotter and the covers felt heavier and heavier, and everything seemed to me to be smelling stronger and stronger of Paul, and I didn't know whether Alan could smell it or not, but it was really oppressing me, I wanted it all to be over.

I pushed him on to his back and moved down on him, kissing his flat belly with the soft fuzz of hair on it, thinking even then how sweet and fresh he tasted, then I took his poor shy cock in my hand and slipped it into my mouth for the first time and as if by magic it started to grow and all of a sudden I felt excited again, and then he gave a little sob and came before he was even fully erect . . .

And that was it, really.

He was all upset of course and said he was sorry and some more about being in love and being in awe and I said it was all right, it was nice, especially the end bit which felt lovely like being in bed with my little brother.

It turned out that that was another wrong thing to say.

One way and another it's a miracle we persevered.

But I think we both knew there were better things to be had.

In the dream I'm walking in the park at dusk. The air is warm and thick and humid, quite difficult to breathe, my throat feels gorged. I am walking under trees and I look up and see these black shapes silhouetted against the sky, like little handbags hanging by their thin black straps from the twigs and branches, hundreds and hundreds of them. And then I notice that some of them are moving, very slowly, hauling themselves up their straps and moving slowly over the branches and clambering over each other with a curious deliberate laborious almost human motion. They have little thin dark wrists and little hands and little impersonal cruel faces, and now some of them are beginning to spread their black leathery wings, slowly, creakily, clumsily, and I understand that they want to fly but they are tethered to their branches for the time being. For the time being I am safe from them, though it's frightening when they flap their wide leathery wings. Now one or two of them have seen me and they are peering down at me. I realise that I have left it rather late. They are almost ready to fly, and when they come they are going to come for me. There are six or seven more trees to walk under before I am clear of them. It is getting darker all the time.

A

Push push push push.

Captain Scarlet all alone, Captain Scarlet far from home.

Young boy goes in strange place.

And still I believed that it would be all right, that that would be the shape of the story. The prince would emerge from underneath his carapace and claim his bride.

Being a man, for me, has always been a bit complex and problematic, ever since puberty really, and the odd thing is that I have never really envied the laddish ones and the rugby hards and that other sort of hard my brother was, and is.

Hard. Well, yes.

Partly her, that she was such a puzzle: mad kid in the gym, dazzling bright defended office lady on her way to work, so open and soft and needy in the bar, and then again a worrying stranger in that dark hot stifling flat, shifty, impatient, holding something back even as she splayed her legs and reached for me. Frightening, a bit, not knowing who the other person is, to realise how very far from home the young boy is . . . I did feel in awe of her.

But it was to do with me as well. To do with being a man. To do with me being a man. See me: I pump the pedals, the tyres hiss on the wet tarmac, I streak through the traffic staring down the stacked taxi drivers. In fencing class, my shoes bounce and shriek on polished wood, I hear my own harsh breath, my steady heartbeat, I feel my partner brace himself, and as he lunges, step into his attack, straight through him, my blade suddenly at his astonished throat. We stop and pull our masks off, his face is red and rueful. He grins in an embarrassed way. I smile in simple pleasure. I have won. Yes, it feels good. Captain Scarlet likes that feeling.

Sex, though, has always seemed a problem: what you do, I mean, a man with a woman. Fucking. What the man does, what I do. It's so intimate, and so aggressive. Some people use it as a way of getting to know someone better: the phrase 'breaking the ice' comes to mind. My brother, if I understand him right, tends to use sex as a way of not getting to know people, though I'd guess they get to know a good deal about him. I've had friends who talk about using their pricks as if they were ignition keys. 'Once I'd got her warmed up . . .' and so on. I can't really bear any of that. And they all talk, men, I mean, other men, as if their pricks are always straining at the leash, eager for release, waiting for the off, all they need is a smile and a nod, no worries mate . . . I know that's not really true, I have access to the relevant literature, I've done the reading, and women tell a very different story from the men: some sexual dysfunction in the early stages of a relationship is very common, so common as to be the norm, almost. First night nerves. Fear of intimacy.

But that can't be it because I *longed* for intimacy. It's the two things, the two things together, the closeness and the violence of it: fucking, what the man does, what I do, it's so intimate, and such an invasion, so bloody *rough*, it seems impossible that they should want us to do that to them, women, girls, to do that awesome thing, how strange it must be, to let yourself be invaded like that, to want to be filled up with our hard hot flesh, to lie there gladly gasping under us, to surrender to, well, Captain Scarlet.

How can I get a hard-on without being a hard?

Because in order to fuck we need to feel strong. And tender is weak.

Soft.

Push push push push. Hissing on wet tarmac. Go go go.

See me. See the man. When I first started teaching I had long hair: for formal occasions I wore it in a ponytail. I baffled the inner-city infants. At first, on my school practice, I would sit and watch the regular teacher, Annie her name was, telling them what to do and trying to show them how to do it, these baffled bleary little buggers who would stumble into school from their chaotic lives at home . . . some of them in particular craved to be touched, they wanted to be stroked and comforted, but I sensed that anything would do, they'd rather be hit than nothing at all. Under Annie's amused sardonic gaze, I was colonised from the very first day by a pair of four-year-old twins, Kyrene and Amalie Hitchens their names were. They both had squints and glasses which made them look even more backward than they were, and they were only sketchily and insecurely house-trained. They were warm damp dirty little girls, and they smelt very strongly of themselves as they sat one on each of my knees staring into my face in this puzzled intent way while Annie read the story. At the end of the afternoon when they had to get down off me and put their coats on and go home, Amalie turned to me and said: 'Are you a man or a lady?'

I love those questions, so much more interesting than the questions adults ask . . . We take them on outings in the summer, trips to wildlife parks and suchlike places supposedly of educational interest. We all get in enormous coaches and the kids are terribly excited, so am I, actually . . . anyway I was sitting next to this kid Thomas Akabusa and I noticed he was frowning as he stared out of the window watching the houses and the trees and that go by, and I said 'What are you thinking about, Thomas?' and he said 'Where's the trip?'

Are you a man or a lady? Where's the trip?

Good questions.

I love teaching little kids. The good bits. I feel as if it makes my thinking strong and simple. Who was it, Bruner, who said that any concept capable of expression could be taught to seven-year-olds? So there's that, trying to do that, the excitement really, of seeing how fast they learn, they learn more by the time they're seven than they'll ever learn afterwards. Making them laugh. Them making me laugh. What they teach me.

And the power, of course. Not to forget that.

I like to tell my classes heroic stories about themselves, how they chartered a coach and went to Scotland to hunt the Loch Ness Monster, and what they took to eat, and what equipment they took for the hunt, and how they set off across the lake, and which of them was rowing and which of them was steering and which of them was looking after Mr Furnace and telling him not to be frightened of the huge waves that would come when the age-old gleaming black flanks of the primeval monster finally heaved themselves up from the dark primordial soup and reared above us in our frail craft, and the brave and ingenious ways in which each of the kids behaved . . . when we're telling these stories I keep asking them what we should do, and most of them are all for killing the monster. Some of the boys and more rarely some of the girls get so carried away that they actually start attacking me as I rear up above them, a pale and weedy monster as monsters go, but infants have an almost infinite capacity for the suspension of disbelief. A few of them, though, are for making friends with it, accommodating it and taming it in some way, and I steer the story in the direction indicated by these gentle ones, these progressive thinkers, towards a peaceful sharing-of-the-planet ending.

Though if it were real, that cold black icy lake, if the creature really came, I wonder if I might be one of the killing party.

Push push push push.

Sometimes the day is miserable, frustrating, the kids thwart me and I thwart myself, but it is never trivial or boring.

My parents found it disappointing, in their different ways, that I wanted to be a primary teacher. *Their* parents were teachers, the first in their families to get higher education. My mother and father went one better. Freddie the user-friendly media professor. Frances the feminist fabulist. And then my brother: Nick the novelist. Oh yes, and then there's Alan, well, he's . . . you know he's fine, he's actually just a primary school teacher, but he loves it! Honestly! State school, yes, inner city! I *know*! He adores it! Like a pig in shit! Secretly, you know, we're *rather proud* of him.

And in a way, they sort of are, not proud exactly, but they have found a way of using me and my work, to shore up their socialist cred. Our son the state school teacher in the inner city. I keep their toehold on reality. I'm their hostage on the front line.

But it isn't really a man's job, is it, teaching such very young children? There must be something . . . strange about a man who . . . I can see it in the eyes of some of my female colleagues, too, they look at me and I'm not like their boyfriends and their husbands, and I worry them.

The fuck with them.

See me. See the man. See Captain Scarlet. Push push push. It'll be OK, I told her. Everything will be OK.

B

He took me to Paris.

I was just so fucking excited when he told me. I went straight in to Desmond and said 'Look Des I've got to have Friday afternoon off and is that all right with you?' and he said 'of course it is my love I'm taking off early myself on Friday', and I restrained myself from saying as per fucking usual, but I couldn't resist hanging voluptuously about in the doorway till he looked up and said 'anything nice, is it?' and I said 'yes actually my lover is taking me to Paris for the weekend'.

I stretched a point. He was not actually my lover at all, and that was crucial.

The Unfuck hung over us like a great dark cloud. The phantom fuck. The fuck we hadn't had. The Unfuck. The Unfuck. Oh, the Unfuck.

It's dark and raining and we have to get our running-away money but Christo the guy who steals the cards is late; he comes stumbling out of the taxi with blood running out of his flat-top and I say 'what's the matter?' and he says 'don't ask, the whole situation's gone nada' and he suddenly sits down on the pavement in the rain and starts moaning, and you're there as well, and you say 'do you think it would be insensitive to ask him if he has the cards?' and I say 'Christo' and he goes 'yeah yeah' and gives me a card. On the card it says Jean Alexander, a name that means nothing to me. We leave Christo sitting propped up under the lamppost and go looking for a cashpoint and find one all lit up like one of those old theatre organs, and there is a girl already there in front of us, a girl in a white mac, and she is tapping lightly on the screen and sort of crooning to it, and all of a sudden a great wodge of damp tenners comes creeping out of the slot and the girl turns and smiles at us and takes her money away into the darkness, and I put the card in, Jean Alexander's card, and the screen lights up and there are all sorts of strange instructions and arrows and options on it that I haven't seen before. I have to choose between Roulette and Babies and Death, and I choose Roulette and the screen goes dark and the machine eats my card, literally eats it, I can see inside where these teeth are biting it up and rolling it round and then it swallows the card and I look at you to see what I should do, and you're frowning and then you say: 'I didn't realise you were a criminal. You must understand, this alters everything.'

I did take a bit of running-away money to Paris, in case I had to run away from my dear one. It was only our third date after all, and there was something about his fierce determined look . . .

But I was thrilled. It was the first time anyone had taken me away just for the sake of it, for the sake of me. Been to quite a few places with Paul of course, but that had always been apropos of one of Paul's things: something to do with movies, something to do with drugs. I always had running-away money or get-home-somehow money in those days of trips with Paul: not so much that I thought I would need to run away from Paul, but some of the people he did business with were the sort of people I didn't fancy owing favours to. And I always felt the possibility that he'd be arrested, or offed, or just do his heart in, and I would have to get home somehow. B. Monkey makes it back to base.

I didn't tell him then, Alan, that his little weekend in Paris was the first proper holiday I'd ever had. I do not count the week in Prestatyn for Deprived Children when I was eleven. I took some running-away money on that and I did run away too, first fucking night, no messing. Back on the doorstep with the milk. I didn't tell him about that either. Too proud. I didn't want his pity. I came on like a trip to Paris for the weekend was a matter of routine for me. But I loved him for doing it, for planning this weekend for the sake of me, me and him, that it was just about that, and nothing to do with long dreary journeys to apartment blocks in the suburbs and walled town houses with guard dogs where I would yawn and snooze the hours away in the hire car outside, being the chick and waiting for the après-deal.

The ferry was good. I'd never been on one before. All the seagulls yelling and the white cliffs as advertised and the bar all warm and smoky and the quick shifty-eyed barmen and we sat up at the bar and drank Ricard which he said was the best for seasickness, and I tossed mine down and put my tongue in his ear, and I could see all the men in the bar wishing they were with me, as well they might. Amazing Beatrice Monkey, read my name. Then up on deck again, the warm bit at the back, and this one big seagull who had decided to come all the way with us, cool and shipwise, slipstreaming in our warm draught like a biker slipstreaming a bus, swooping and soaring and showing us his moves, and once he came really close and I saw his mad eyes and I thought Bruno.

Damage, damage, there's been so much damage, I hope it hasn't warped me out of shape. One of the books we did for A level at the Institute was Ernest Hemingway's *A Farewell to Arms* and in that book he says the world breaks everyone and afterwards we're strong in the broken places, he is talking about psychic damage, hurts to the heart, and shit I hope he's right, but his analogy is one of broken bones and that's not actually true, some fuck from Neasden bust my collarbone with a tyre lever once and though it grew a great big lump of bone around the broken place it isn't stronger there, it's weaker.

I saw him burning.

The French train with its different smell, its slippery plastic seats. Getting closer to the Gare du Nord, the cloud of Unfuck starting again to settle round us. The echoing Metro, shadowy faces and the glitter of white tiles, dark when we came out, the street with market stalls, the bright lights bouncing off fruit and fish, and then through the tiny entrance to the Hotel de la Merde, its yellowy piss-coloured walls inside, the ratfaced tart behind her tiny toffee-coloured counter checking us out with her small eyes, and in no time there we were trudging up another carpeted stairway, narrow and steep this time, with a cold black metal handrail, and it was half excitement and elation at having found it, made it, got there, and half agonbite of Unfuck sitting heavy on our shoulders and digging its nails in deep.

The sheets were cold and clammy nylon, also faintly yellowy: this tour was clearly sponsored by Cheapo Cheapo Productions and I told myself this is OK because it is more personal, my dear one is a poor man, but what he has, it's all for me, and I shucked off me chemise fast as a fucking fish, trying not to think, my head buzzing, hearing him gasp at seeing my white body so suddenly there I suppose, then into the clammy pit, and God it was chilly, and I was going 'hurry up, hurry up, I'm fucking freezing here' and he was looking slightly baffled and anxious and I suddenly thought, we haven't discussed this, have we, maybe there's a different way, maybe the straight people do it different. I mean Paul in a new place would always make his call to touch base then take a shot or do a line and *then* mark the mattress, but honestly, here we were two eager young things with no business commitments and no narcotic imperatives and no agenda really but nooky, what had I missed out, were we supposed to do six laps of the Louvre first or what?

The thoughts that rattle through a young girl's head as she awaits the coming of her lover.

The sheets were so chilly I was sure they must be damp as well, but love conquers all, doesn't it, two hot young bodies can work wonders, but when Alan slipped in he was shivering, cold as a salmon, and courting doom again by whispering again how it would be OK.

And it was not OK, it wasn't, it was not OK, it was Unfuck, I had thought after the first time well one consolation is it's never going to be as bad as this again, but oh it was worse, Unfuck is not just an absence, it's an evil presence, and so hurtful, and I started to hate him a little because I thought he must hate me somewhere deep down or why would he shrink into himself like this and . . . cringe from the minge, when all I wanted was to make us both happy, and I exhausted myself to fretfulness stroking and sucking and kissing and rubbing my pretty tits all over him, and then he mumbled something about it was because he loved me too much, and I said in that case I wished he loved me a bit less and then we might have some fun, and he turned his cold back and stared at the wall and I started to cry, and I couldn't stop. I thought I had got right out of crying and now he had got me into it again. He turned and put his arms around me and begged me to stop, which was stupid because he was crying too. And I couldn't stop, I couldn't.

We were trapped with each other. Between those clammy sheets, in that sad bed, in that mustard-coloured cell. And I looked over at my bag squatting on the shit-brown table by the door, and I was glad I had brought my running-away money.

A

It was as if there was nothing else.

We trudged doggedly along the banks of the Seine like a couple of lifers in the exercise yard. I was aching for her, aching for her, and my cock felt like a shrivelled leaf.

Who sets these tortures up for us?

Notre Dame loomed up in front of us, a great dark lump, we stood in its chilling shadow, and she stared at it as if she were frightened of it, as if she were in Class One and it was the Loch Ness Monster. Her dismay was infectious. We were frightened of Paris.

We tried the Pompidou and it tied our tongues. We stood in front of Meret Oppenheim's fur cup and saucer and nothing happened to us. People skittered past chattering and laughing and pointing things out to each other in an assortment of bright languages, some of them giving us the odd sharp birdy glance: look at the dumb, numb English animals. Outside in the square it was cold: we stood for twenty minutes watching a mime who fixed us with his dark and glittering eye: his thing was stillness, so that when he made his tiny movements it was like the flicker of a snake's tongue. There was something intimate and disgusting about his performance, something insulting about it: he had, I felt, some terrible message for us personally. I asked her if she wanted to go and she said she didn't care whether she went or not. Eventually he fixed his glittering eye on someone else.

Walking, walking. I tried to take her photograph and she kept shying away. I have some of those photographs still – the back of her neck, the swirl of her coat. There is one in which you can see her face. She looks like a trapped animal.

We . . .

I don't want to go on with this. It's too – days can be so terribly long, so . . .

We . . .

What is worst is the feeling that this is what it's really like, this is how it really is, between people I mean, and the rest is all pretending and whistling in the dark.

All the time I was telling her come on, it's going to be OK, really, and oh God asking her what the matter was when it was obvious what the matter was, it was me.

It's going to be OK, really, it's going to be OK. Look at my face, see my terrified grin. Of course it's going to be OK.

Why can't I stop thinking about Paris now? That's . . . long ago, that's long gone.

I don't have to think about Paris. We are here now. She is living with me here, in Shepherds Bush. I can look out of the window. Roofs. Clouds. The swifts wheel and tumble.

She lies safe in my arms, she loves me in her sleep, I am with her in her dreams, she tells me so.

But I don't know where she goes or what she does.

Which day was it? Tuesday. I was sitting here, on the sofa by the window, just . . . watching the clouds, and she came in grinning and without a word she climbed on top of me and started kissing me and rubbing herself against me, and I . . . caught a handful of her hair, and buried my nose in her neck, and caught a faint whiff of cigarette smoke, and something else, something I didn't recognise or couldn't place, and then forgot about it, forgot everything except her breathless: *'Inside! Inside!'*

It's going to be OK. It's going to be OK. Everything is going to be OK.

B

I found that I couldn't run away from him after all because it was like we were both trapped in it together – I wished we could both run away from each other together, but that doesn't make sense, does it? I thought: that's almost a joke, I'll tell him and make him laugh, maybe we could even have a little laugh about the Unfuck, but I took one look at him and thought forget about that, this guy looks ready to be shot.

One thing about abroad, it always seems to get dark sooner. We went out into the night and the street market was still going and it looked pretty. We went into a cheapish looking restaurant and sat down and tried to understand the handwritten menu. We both ordered duck but when it came it was a little fan of slimy bleeding slices out of some poor duck's chest with a great frill of fat on each slice. More or less raw, and more or less cool. And as we had nothing else to do and nothing else to talk about but Unfuck, we sat and ate this raw duck's fat chest until it was all gone. The restaurant was practically empty but they had put us at this tiny little table for two, so small that our faces were practically touching which would I suppose have been fine, very nice for the two young lovers, had it not been for the Unfuck. And the duck.

So we sat, nose to nose, squelching this raw fat duck's chest between our jaws, while the hooknosed French waiter probed a boil on the back of his neck and watched us with interest and contempt, from time to time inviting his pus-faced female colleague to look at the English fucks who would eat any fucking shit you cared to set before them, raw poultry a speciality. (One of these days I'm going back there: catch the

77

terror in the French fuck's eye as Beatrice Monkey bursts, boots first, through his rotting portals.)

It seemed to be hard to talk. Not just hard to think of things to say and ways to say them. Hard to form the words. Hard to make the sounds. It was as if I couldn't remember how you worked out the business of talking and eating and breathing, which bit you did when. It was very hot in the restaurant and someone seemed to be extracting most of the oxygen from the air. After a bit the room started to lurch from side to side, and then it started to loom and recede as well. I realised that I was feeling a bit strange, and I asked Alan if we could please just fuck off now, and he said OK but seemed to take several hours staring at his francs and trying to work out the tip till I said 'leave them fucking nothing' and I do remember lurching towards the door and heading back to Hotel de la Merde and hauling myself up that narrow ginger staircase, then stumbling through the door across the room into the bathroom to hug the toilet in a passionate embrace and release that first effortless cascade of half-chewed duck red wine Unfuck and misery. At last, at last, I had something to do in Paris, I could not fuck but by golly I could puke and shit, and that is what I set about doing in that nightmare bathroom conveniently tiled from floor to ceiling, ideal for serious torture it would have been, with a huge bandy-legged bath for electrical games and repetitive near-drowning, and an uneven floor with a drain in the middle to hose the blood and shit and puke away.

Down on that cold tiled floor, hugging my trusty toilet pal, that was where I spent the rest of our holiday in Paris, with briefer periods in the clammy bed.

After the first riotous explosions I felt briefly better, better enough to feel embarrassed at him having seen me in such straits, but he was OK about it, better than OK in fact, he was tender and solicitous and unsqueamish beyond the call of duty and I started to like the gloomy shy-pricked sod again, he was so kind to me, so kind to me, leaning over me and holding my head and telling me he was there for me and he was looking after me, and I let him, I let him wipe my little girly face and lead me back to bed and prop me up against the pillows.

He asked me if I'd like him to read me a story, and I asked him if he would tell me one instead, and he did.

The story he told me was about a girl called Beatrice who wanted to see the world. She would stare into the windows of travel agents and look at the pictures of foreign parts. The ones she liked best were islands, small islands with white sandy beaches round the edges and dark green forests in the middle. She really wanted to go and live on an island like that, this girl Beatrice, but she didn't have the money.

Then one day when she was moaning on about islands to the office cat, to her amazement the cat said: so you want to see an island? Fine. I'll send you to an island.

He was talking in this soft sleep voice, Alan, and it was more like being in a dream than being told a story. I thought, he's done this before, and then I stopped thinking and I just went into the story and let it hold me and carry me.

The cat told Beatrice to lie down on the floor and close her eyes, and she did that, and felt the floor strong and solid under her holding the weight of her body, and then she felt herself growing lighter and lighter. She opened her eyes and saw that she was floating above the office. She could look down and see them all typing and on the phone and taking good meetings and drinking Sancerre and eating the sandwiches they'd sent her out for. And then she became lighter still and floated right up to the ceiling, and then passed right through the ceiling and on up through the roof, and then she was out, floating in the cold air over London high above the houses and offices and the grey glittering snake of the river, and then she started to move horizontally, silently and very fast, gradually accelerating and skimming over the land, then the sea, the blue wrinkled channel with its tiny boats, then more land, green and brown and whitey-grey where there were mountains, then a huge expanse of sea, enormous, calm, and empty, and the cool air started to get warmer, and the breeze dropped, and she realised that she was going very slowly now, and when she looked down she realised that she was hovering over a little island in the middle of the enormous ocean; an island with white sandy beaches round the edges, and a dark green forest in the middle.

She felt herself descending very gently, the air getting warmer and warmer all the time, and then she was lying on the white sand at the water's edge. It was real. The sand was warm and dry. She picked up a handful and let it trickle through her fingers. The sea was calm; little waves shushed gently, unfolding, stretching, and running softly back into themselves. She took off her dress and walked into the sea and it was cool and tingly and then warm, and she swam and she rolled and she floated in the water and let it rub itself all over her until she felt clean, clean, clean, and then she came out of the water and stood on the beach and let the sun dry her.

Then six monsters came out of the dark green forest. They were green and grey in colour and their shapes were indeterminate and indescribable. But they were big, as big as cathedrals. They stood in a row in front of Beatrice.

Who are you, and what do you want? said Beatrice.
    We are the forest monsters, and we eat girls, said the monsters. Who are you?
    My name is Beatrice and I tame monsters, said Beatrice. Besides, I am too thin and tough to eat. My suggestion is we form a gang and muck about to our heart's content.
    We don't know how to muck about, said the monsters shyly.
    In that case, I had better be your leader, said Beatrice. Get in a line, shortest at the front, tallest at the back.

The forest monsters recognised immediately that they were in the presence of a superior life form. They spent the whole of that day mucking about in the sea, mucking about on the sand, and mucking about in the forest in accordance with Beatrice's instructions, and by the time the sun went down they were all so tired that they fell asleep in a heap on top of each other.

And Beatrice went to sleep too, feeling very happy. She had found her island and tamed her monsters, and she lived happily ever after and never went back to the office again.

*

There was just this one table lamp on in the room. Alan was sitting in the one armchair between the table and the bed. His face was all shadows but the light was full on his arms and the hairs on his arms looked golden in the light, not brown. It was nice having a story told about me. It was nice being made to feel like a little girl. I thought he's a funny sort of lover, but he'd make a fucking brilliant big sister. Then I drifted into sleep, I felt so weak and floaty.

And woke again God knows when in pitch blackness with a pain in my gut like someone twisting a knife and I got out of bed and I couldn't find the bathroom door and then when I did find it I couldn't find the light and I started to vomit but oh God liquid shit started to run out of me at the same time and there was nothing really I could do about it but hang on to the pan like someone in a shipwreck and wait for it all to stop.

But it took so long that I was too weak to move by the time it had finished, and I thought that I was going to die there in my own mess on the white tiles of that cruel bathroom, but he came in, my sweet one, and he wiped me down and cleaned me up and carried me back to bed and held my hand until I slept again, and when I woke in the morning he was still holding my hand.

He seemed happy to be there. He was smiling at me. I thought this is a bit weird, we haven't had sex yet but already he's wiping my bottom on the third date. What sort of relationship have I got myself into? Then I thought of a joke: I know this was supposed to be a dirty weekend but this is ridiculous. He sort of laughed but I got the feeling he felt it was unworthy of the occasion. I said, what I mean is, sorry about all this. He said listen, there is nowhere else I would rather be now, and no one else I would rather be with. I love you, he said, that's what it is. I wanted to say how can you love me, you don't know anything about me, but that seemed rather an odd thing to say in the circumstances, so I didn't.

After a bit he got up and went downstairs and caused Ratface to call a doctor for me, which was very clever of him I thought. I was starting to feel better all the time, but very weak. The doctor was disconcertingly young and tasty, and very nice with it, spoke English, everything. He was very worried that I was having such an unhappy experience of Paris. Then he gave me a couple of shots in the bottom and a bottle of pills, took most of our money, and fucked off with a Gallic smile.

I did some more sleeping. Alan went for a walk and something to eat, came back. In the afternoon he gave me a bath, quite suspiciously skilfully, and I got back into bed and did some more sleeping. When I woke up it was evening again, and I felt well enough to totter out into the night for a coffee and a bun. I had to hold tight to Alan all the time I was walking. I felt like tissue paper.

We went back to the room and as soon as he opened the door I could smell this horrible smell of puke and diarrhoea and old sweat and just well illness I suppose and I thought God no wonder the doctor wrinkled up his nose when he came in, and I said to Alan God I'm sorry and how can you stand it, and he said I don't mind it, why should I, it's you. I said listen I have to ask you this – it's not the main interest or anything is it, I mean you're not going to require me to shit myself every night are you because I'm not sure I could hack that even though I've done pretty well in that line so far. I was joking of course but he took me seriously and said it wasn't that, that what it was was love. Then he undressed me and put me to bed, and undressed himself, and held me in his arms all night, and I had such a good deep sleep, such a good deep good deep sleep.

Incompatible, clearly. I should have run from such smug lunatic sweetness.

I can't say no, I can't walk away, I can't do it. Trapped by his despotic fantasies.

He thinks I am magical but I am ordinary.

Ordinary for me but not for him. Oh shit I can't resist it I'm not strong enough not to feed on the love in his eyes I want more and more I want him to praise me praise me Beatrice Monkey beautiful animal crazy sister strange little bride I worship your wiry little worked-out body; oh B. Monkey your eyes are fire your hair is angelfur your snot is made of emeralds your shit is liquid gold.

yeah say it say it cos I can't get enough of it

tell me you would die for me

yeah cos they all would

Beatrice Monkey read my name!

I was in this gym, not a flash one, it was like a school one with wall-bars and stuff and we were climbing over this big padded box thing and the idea was you wriggle along the top and then slide off it head first without using your hands and I was with Mick and Damon and they had already done it, they were both lying on this big gym mattress looking up at me and telling me come on it was easy – I was a bit worried about falling on my face and bruising it but if I pressed my legs tight against it as I wriggled down that gave me some control. The only thing was that my knickers were coming down with the friction. My bum was right out of them and I was hoping that the boys hadn't noticed – they were both wearing black shell suits all zipped up – but then I thought it feels quite nice I don't really care and I was starting to feel a bit sexy and I said catch me and I let myself slither all the way down and they were laughing and stretching their arms out to catch me.

I opened my eyes and there were his eyes very close looking into my eyes as if he could see right inside me and liked what he saw and I said hello, and he took my hand and put it on his cock and it was really big and hard and I thought a miracle, a miracle, let's see, and put my leg up over his hip and tried, and found not altogether to my surprise that I was wet already, and in two seconds all our troubles were over, it just slipped in as if it knew its way, lovely and warm and steady and strong, and we just lay there face to face for ages it felt like, hardly moving at all, not needing to, it was so sharp and vivid, the feeling of it, so . . . *detailed* really, so, well, so absolutely satisfactory that I started laughing out loud in this little weak hoarse voice which was all my puking exploits seemed to have left me with, and he said: 'what's funny?' and I said 'we are'. He asked me if it was all right, if I was well enough, and I said yes, yes, just what the doctor ordered.

A

She is absolutely and unconditionally perfect for me and there are things that I can hardly bear about her.

Some of the things that I can hardly bear about her are the things that put me totally in thrall.

Her sudden eruptions of hysterical arrogance: Beatrice Monkey read my name, all that . . . I mean, honestly, really, like some – like one of those faked-up films that . . . She actually took me once and showed me this wall – it was near Royal Oak Station on the run-in to Paddington, where the huge panting 125s slide in from Wales and Cornwall. The wall was the back of a grimy terrace that looked directly out on to the railway and it was covered with graffiti, faces, slogans, dismaying messages like punches in the face: NIGGERS OUT, DEATH TO SALMAN RUSHDIE, KILL IRISH SHIT, BRING ME THE HEAD OF DAVID PERKINS and so on, but many more obscure but obviously unique identifying signatures, most of them executed in a bold swirling style, many of them overlaying each other, many of them whitewashed over but still faintly visible, some of them so faint that I imagined their perpetrators might be respectable citizens now, with paunches and mortgages and teenage kids they didn't understand. And over them all, white-washed out but still clearly visible, so high on the wall that it was difficult to think how it could have been executed:

B. MONKEY READ MY NAME!

I didn't know what to say.

Oh, I could find sentences about the athleticism that must have been involved in getting up there, the confidence and bouncy flair of the swirling line ... but somehow I couldn't bring myself to say them. My chest felt choked with anger. I didn't know why. At the pointlessness of it, the desperate pathetic self-promotion, the mindless misuse of energy and talent ... I wanted to clout her one across her earhole. And then I looked at her and her face was so eager, and I thought she's like one of my little kids showing me her picture, it doesn't matter if I don't understand, what she wants is recognition that I see her work, that I see *her*, and I thought what a silly fucking fool I am, and I said: 'brilliant' and though I can't explain it even to myself I meant it.

Maybe we all want the world to read our names.

My fucking father certainly does. Professor Freddie Furnace. Read his name in the refereed journals, read his name in *Who's Who*, read his name among the credits on the flickering screen. My mother too. Four times winner of The Other Award, named as consultant for every other right-on reading scheme. My brother Nick once told me he wanted to write his name across the literary history of the late twentieth century. What a prick. I told Beatrice about that and she said he sounded like a boy she knew from Acton who liked to write his name on people's chests with a Stanley knife.

But I'm not like that. I've never wanted to be famous. Where would I want to write my name?

On her. On her. On her.

And never be obliterated.

So what does that say about me?

What a strange life she has had. And yet she laughs at me when I say this and says my childhood was the strange one. Two parents, regular school, always plenty of money ... it's true of course. I never thought of my childhood as privileged but who does? I went short of love and she went short of everything else.

'My mother has a personality style of unremitting sadness.'

That was something she said to me – I think she read it in a book. She said it rather proudly.

I piece what I can together of the scraps she throws me. She remembers hardly anything about her father, a big man who carried her on his shoulders, gave her a rabbit, gave her mother something to cry about, and fucked off for good before my dear one even started school. For years she used to look at tall men with curly hair in the street, wondering if they might be her daddy. She longs for him still, I think, longs to be carried on his shoulders, longs for his unique and unconditional love. She has mine, she has mine, the bastard should have stuck around long enough so that she could get disillusioned with him. Every girl I have ever known has been screwed up about her father one way or another.

'Praise me, praise me!' She sucks it up, she can't get enough of it, she thinks she is the only one that didn't get enough praise.

She was a good and clever girl at primary school and then she got lost and terrified in the cavernous echoing slum of a secondary school that was all there was to go to. Stayed at home reading books, she said, her mother too soft to push her into going to school, well, all the better probably, most of the kids I teach go backwards after they reach the age of twelve . . . she fell in love with a guy who did a milk round then, and took to going round with him, a sort of phantom father, Eddie his name was. She says nothing but nice things about him: that he was kind and funny and gave her good feelings about herself, the sex was something she hardly thought about, something she 'took in her stride har har' (I *hate* those coarse reductive one-liners she comes out with still, about such delicate material too) but as Eddie was thirty-seven years old to her thirteen, the shit rather hit the fan when the School Attendance Officer got round to the case of Beatrice Monkey.

She was dealt with rather sensitively, unlike poor Eddie, who got two years (and serve the bastard right). An educational psychologist pronounced her school-phobic and emotionally disturbed, and prescribed for her an alternative educational strategy. (She saw, and sees, school phobia as an entirely normal condition: in her opinion schoolophiles are the ones in need of treatment, and I think she might be right.) Anyway, the alternative educational strategy first tried was individual tuition in the home. The individual home tutor, as so often happens, turned out to be someone who was severely frightened of schools himself and indeed most other adults, and the only subject that really interested him was himself and his problems, which he felt could be resolved, with Beatrice's cooperation, by the same means used by Eddie the milkman. But his personality, unlike Eddie's, was highly unattractive. He was spurned, and fled.

As a last resort she was enrolled in an experimental unit run by one of those crazy urban-action charities that were still around a few years ago: street theatre cum group therapy cum city farm cum commune, that sort of thing. The school unit catered for teenagers who were too scared or too weird or too rebellious to go to school, or so disruptive that though they loved it at school the school refused to let them in. Only extreme examples of each category. Only twelve kids altogether. All in the same room. Near-autistics to near-psychopaths. A recipe for disaster, I would have said, but she loved it, made friends with the wild animals, discovered her own wildness, and came out of it with five good GCEs and a wide circle of criminal contacts. She was there for just over a year. The woman who ran it must have been brilliant; but she went off to be brilliant somewhere else, as brilliant people will, and the whole thing folded.

She was only sixteen.

She doesn't seem to want to talk too much about the next few years. She was in work a little and out of it a lot, she knew a lot of people and she did a lot of things, some of them stupid. Something happened that gave her a bit of a shock, and she decided to change her life. She went to evening classes, got two A levels and learnt shorthand and typing FUCKING FAST SPEEDS TOO YOU BETTER BELIEVE IT READ MY NAME and got this job as a secretary ASSISTANT ASSISTANT FUCK-

ING ASSISTANT BABY WATCH MY RISE TO FAME AND FORTUNE in this quite successful little independent film production company. But what really happened in those missing years? It doesn't take six years to write your name on a few walls. You don't want to know, my dear one, she says. I'm here now. Aren't I?

After we had managed to manage, with the sex, she told me all about agonbite of Unfuck and running-away money and how desperate she had been not to have her sad lonely unfucked image recorded by my trusty Ricoh FF9. She was still, comically, slightly anxious that I might be a man who only got his rocks off on sickies. Couldn't see at first that what I got my rocks off on was absolute trust and love. She just, I don't know, trusted me. She just gave herself. Is this unusual? I just don't know. No, I think it doesn't matter, whether it's unusual or not that is, I don't give a fuck whether we are usual or not so long as we are happy. But it's funny, that no one knows how the other people are with each other. I didn't use to talk like this, I didn't use to think like this. She has broken my immune system, she has invaded my vocabulary.

Yeah you fuckers read my name!

Now I've embarrassed myself.

Hey look, we had such a time that summer after we cracked the ice in Paris. She was working at the film company and me teaching my little kids. She kept a toehold in that strange hot smoky flat in Battersea, but four or five nights a week she would come and sleep in my little room in Shepherds Bush. It was a top-floor room, sloping ceilings, with a tiny kitchen bit and bathroom bit. A little letterbox of a window; you could stand and look out and see a jumble of roofs and chimneys and tops of trees and the swifts wheeling. Lovely, really. I would get home an hour or so before she did, pound up the stairs all red and sweaty carrying my bike, push push push push, pull off my clothes, stumbled into my tiny cupboard of a bathroom and stand under the shower, a feeble trickle but cool enough to soothe my pounding brain. Pull a pair of shorts on and wait for her to come, trying to work, unable to concentrate, listening, sniffing the air almost, willing her down the street and through the door and up the stairs.

And I would jump every time, my heart bouncing, as the handle turned and her head came round the door, her bright painted smile, for a moment a disconcerting stranger, the slick office lady, then she'd be across the room to me, and we would bump clumsily together grabbing at each other, she'd always feel so hot, and her heart going as fast as a bird's, and we'd kiss, sucking at each other's faces, licking each other, her lovely hot salty upper lip . . . I remember that first time she came round to me straight from work, sliding my hand under her full cotton skirt, feeling her bare legs so cool and smooth and then cupping my hand over the hot bulge at the front of her pants and she gave a little squeak and then hissed: '*In*side! *In*side!' in a fierce urgent whisper, as if it was a matter of life or death, and I slipped my fingers into her and she draped her arms around my neck and rode wriggling on my fingers, laughing, panting, licking my nose . . .

I told her it would be OK, and it was, eventually.

Waking in the morning is favourite, just as it was that first time we managed in Paris. Watching her sleep, then watching her wake. Sometimes I watch her dreaming. I had read about the rapid eye movements we make when we're dreaming but I had never seen them before I started sleeping with Beatrice. Her eyelids are dark, darker than the olive of her cheeks, with thick lashes, and when she dreams her eyelids tremble almost imperceptibly but very quickly, and sometimes her mouth moves too, but slowly, clumsily, druggily, hopelessly trying to keep up with her racing brain. Little glimpses of her teeth. Sometimes little glimpses of the whites of her eyes. Her steady breathing. Her steady heartbeat. Her warm skin. Awesome, mysterious – another presence there by my side. Who is she when she dreams, where is she? The rapid eye movements usually only last a few seconds at a time. I woke her once, when her eyelids had stopped flickering, and asked her if she had been dreaming and she told me an extraordinarily lengthy and convoluted narrative that began with some sort of accident, then went on to a complicated struggle with a cashpoint machine, and a cast of characters I had never heard of, and then she smiled and said 'you were there too', then squeezed my hand and fell fast asleep again.

She loves me in her sleep.

Sometimes, not often, she wakes first. I open my eyes and find myself nose to nose with her, so close it's blurry, breathing each other's breath, her eyes so close it feels as if I am actually somehow inside their bright brown radiance, and I feel rather than see her smile. Our bare bodies touching all along their length. Feeling the warmth of her body doing me good, making me strong. Feeling my drowsy prick wake, stir, rise against her, and she reaches down and takes it in her hand and brushes it gently against the lips of her vagina.

'Inside! Inside!'

Young boy goes in strange place.

And sometimes I wake and she's not there.

Am I a man or a lady? Where's the trip?

B

Ah fuck it was just an impulse. I wanted to share it with him, just a little spin, just a little outing. I'd done it once or twice on my own, since I'd been with him, couldn't resist it, just for the feel of it, just a little slip-in, just a little cruise around, park it on.a double yellow, call a cab and safe home, no harm done to anyone, just to satisfy that little bit of wild, just my little secret. Anyone would understand, I thought.

It was so hot that evening, six p.m. and the air like soup, sun struggling through the rainbow fumes, feet throbbing in the high-heel black stilettos, I'd only walked fifty yards and I could feel the sweat gathering between my tits, I saw the guy leave his dark green Daimler on the corner of Clarendon and go in Shapero's the bookshop, I thought he's good for ten minutes and I only want one and a half, I am fucked if I am walking home tonight.

You should really dress right to nick a nice car and I was very smart that day. I did it my special girly way that Damon showed me, it's very flash, and you can do it with loads of people about. You lean against the car like you're all bored and irritated waiting for your bloke, and that tells you if it's alarmed or not. Then, *still* leaning against it, you hairpin the fucker *with your back to it*, it's not so hard because it's all touch anyway. Then you look at your watch and pretend you've run out of time, turn round and pretend to open the door with a key, and in you get.

I started the engine, lovely deep whispery purr, and eased out into Clarrie and wiggled up and down the one-ways all the way through to St Marks and Quintin and North Pole then round

Wood Lane and down to Shepherds Bush that way with the air conditioning on full blast and the lovely leathery smell, then round to the flat, nipped out and rang the bell.

Alan came down looking anxious and I laughed and said I'd come to take him for a ride. I said I'd borrowed the car from a friend. He got in, and I took him a little cruisy ride along the A40, cool and glidey, Beatrice Monkey at the controls. So serene, like our own cool room in the hot desperate evening. He kept looking at me and I knew he was wondering who this friend was who would have such a gorgeous car and lend it to a mad fuck like me. But he didn't ask, and I wasn't volunteering. I was having a nice time and I think he was.

I asked him if he'd like to have a drive and he said he wouldn't mind, so I stopped in a layby and we changed places. He was a dead careful driver, both hands on the wheel, all that, glance in the mirror every two seconds. And he was a bit nervous of the power of the thing. But he relaxed after a while, stopped holding the wheel so hard, managed to talk at the same time even.

'Afraid I'm not such a brilliant driver as you,' he said.
  'You're all right,' I said.
  'No,' he said. 'Took me three goes to pass the test. What about you?'
  'Never took one,' I said.

He thought I was joking.

I lifted my skirt up and let the breeze cool me. Then I took off my knickers. 'This is power steering,' I told him. 'You can drive this car with two fingers.'

After a while we took a few turns and found a field.

It was lovely.

The sun was going down and we stopped at a pub, sort of a classy semi-restaurant place, and went in for a beer. I was sitting so I could see out of the window to the car park. Eventually he said: 'Look, I've had a wonderful time, I mean I'm *having* a wonderful time. But I do keep wondering whose car we're in. I mean you don't have to tell me if it's private.'

I said I would love to tell him if only I knew, but I didn't have the faintest fucking idea whose car we'd borrowed.

See his face.

'I don't believe you,' he said. Over his shoulder I saw a man parking an XJ10 right next to the Daimler. He got out of it and walked towards the restaurant entrance with his girlfriend. Just right.

'Come on,' I said to Alan. 'Let's go home.'

In the car park, I leaned against the XJ10 and opened it the same way as I had done the Daimler. Alan was standing there staring at me in this appalled way.

'Come on, get in,' I said.

'We can't do that,' he said.

'Please,' I said. 'I think it's best. They might be looking for the other one by now.'

'You mean you really stole it?'

"Borrowed it! Borrowed it! Come on, get the fuck in!'

I must have sounded a bit savage I suppose. Well I was on edge. Amazing lot of people get caught because they hang round on the scene arguing about something.

'No,' he said.

'Oh, come on Alan, what are you going to do, catch a fucking bus?'

'Yes, maybe I will,' he said.

'Look, please,' I said. 'I'm going in this. Please. Come with me, keep me company. It's just a game, Alan. We're not hurting their cars. They'll get them back.'

He got in, I got it started, and I drove him back to Shepherds Bush. Neither of us said a word all the way.

It's not just a game, of course, it's a drug, it's better than a drug, almost as good as sex, amazingly good *with* sex . . . or indeed drugs.

But it was clear that crime was not something I could share with my dear one, even harmless stuff like t.d.a.

What I must do, of course, is give it up entirely, and I will. I *will*. What I have with Alan is becoming – maybe has already become – too good to lose.

A

She kept a toehold in that strange hot smoky flat in Battersea, but four or five nights a week ... she kept a toehold in that strange hot smoky flat in Battersea, but ... she kept a toehold in that flat in Battersea, she kept a toehold.

This man called Paul. He owned the flat, he let her live there. It wasn't long before I realised that there must be more to it than that. I'm not a complete innocent. People have leftover bits of their lives. We learn to love by loving, we all have people in our pasts. Paul I guessed was one of the mistakes she had made, and Beatrice is odd about her mistakes. I think she's proud of them.

I hate mistakes.

One night, I met him, Paul. We were going to this pasta place in Battersea Park Road just round the corner from his flat, and she asked me if I minded if she nipped in to get some clean knickers and a shirt to wear for work next day. Of course I said no and we walked up these wide shallow stairs with their old gold carpet that seemed to tug at our feet like quicksand.

It was dark inside the flat, all the curtains were drawn shut. The same close, hot, dusty smell, old ashtrays, but something else. Some sort of scent or aftershave, and yes, someone had been smoking a joint too.

'Paul?' she said, and he came out of one of the bedrooms. He was a tall thin guy, quite old, at least forty-five I would have said. Black shiny hair slicked back. White shirt, dark trousers.

'We're not stopping, I just came by to get some knickers,' she said. 'This is Alan.'

Then she went out. I couldn't help noticing that the bedroom she went into was the one Paul had just come out of.

Paul shook hands with me.

'Nice to meet you, Alan,' he said, then paused and frowned. Neither of us seemed to be able to think of anything to say.

'Are you in the business?' he asked, finally.

'Which business?'

He smiled.

'I don't know, Alan. Whatever.'

'I'm a teacher,' I said.

It seemed to galvanise him.

'Good God! A teacher! I'm staggered. What do you teach?'

'Everything, to very small children.'

'That's beautiful,' he said. 'I approve of that very much indeed.' He looked at me thoughtfully for a few moments.

'Would you like a go on my piano?' he said.

'I don't play the piano,' I said.

'So you don't teach them fucking music then,' he said.

'I play guitar a bit,' I said.

'You play, and they sing. Right? Is that right?'

'That's right,' I said.

'Well,' he said. 'Tonight, *I'll* play and *you* can sing. How's that?'

He went and sat down at the piano with the framed photographs and started immediately to play some chords. He was not a good player but he could play chords. He put them out in a slightly broken irregular rhythm that nevertheless had a kind of style to it. It sounded like Cole Porter but I couldn't place the song.

'You know this?' he said.

'No, I don't think so,' I said.

'Come on, of course you fucking know it,' he said. 'Come on, don't be shy, sing it.'

Beatrice came out of the bedroom.

'Stop pissing about, Paul, I told you we weren't stopping,' she said.

Paul went on playing. Now I could recognise the song.

'Come on, then,' she said to me.

'Sorry,' he said to me. 'You mustn't mind me. I enjoyed meeting you, Alan.'

He went on playing his jagged little chords.

'Are you all right, Paul?' she said. She sounded tender, and I felt a stab of jealousy.

'I'm fine,' he said, and smiled rather a sweet smile.

'OK then,' she said. 'We're off now.'

But he had got to the end of the song before she moved.

B

That was the night they came round and hurt Paul and broke everything in the apartment. His poor piano, and all his photographs. They must have seen us going in, and coming out. They were probably just waiting for us to leave before they went in.

He owed them money, of course. He's such a fool to himself, Paul, and so arrogant with it. People get enraged with him. Why I loved him, partly.

I go back a long way with Paul. I even knew him in the days of wild. We even had each other once in those days, just, you know, to see. But I was only a kid then, and that was how he saw me, a mad kid, though a reliable business contact. On the whole, though, we moved in very different circles.

Then years later, after I had become a respectable law-abiding citizen, he walked into the office one day, and it turns out that he actually *is* a film director, though not a remotely bankable one. Still he could take meetings and lunches with the best of them, in fact that day he managed to talk Desmond into setting up a little development deal that came to nothing in the end, and on his way out he pulled me for a quick lunch in Julie's, as it happened.

He had a room free in his apartment, and I was desperate at the time to break away from Carl, so we made a deal there and then. Paul had his car on a meter, we went round to Carl's place – he was out, fortunately – got my clothes and tapes and took them straight round to Prince of Wales Drive and sealed it with a second bottle of Roederer and a rather slow sleepy shag that very afternoon. I phoned in to the office and told Desmond that someone I'd had at lunch had agreed with me all too well, which was taking a bit of a risk I suppose, but he likes having this outrageous assistant he can tell anecdotes about to the makers, breakers, shakers, fakers and liberty takers he gives telephone to all day. 'Good little worker, too, she is,' he always finishes up. 'Fucking fast speeds, you better believe it. All right, darling.' *Click.*

I like being a mad bugger too, I must admit it. Being it, and boasting about it. Even now . . . I'm a fucking disaster, aren't I? What will become of me?

A

She's mine now. She lives with me. She is my girlfriend. her past is immaterial. And so is mine.

Yesterday when I was waiting for her to come home I started clearing the shelves, to make more space for her, for her books and things. Her Poe, her Dostoevsky and her James M. Cain, her doomy old heavy metal tapes.

There was stuff on the top shelf I never knew I'd kept. Old college essays, old pure maths textbooks full of desperate underlining and hopeless yellow highlighting. And then, with a dizzying lurch like vertigo, I turned over a small bundle of letters in Babbie's round girlish hand, and a green A4 file. I tipped the file and she slid out into my lap and gazed reproachfully up at me.

What happened in the end with me and Babbie puzzles me still. After the accusations, after the sobbing, after the wine-tasting, things went quiet at home. She wasn't mentioned again by either of my parents for the remainder of the vacation. My mother developed a new line of terrible silences at the dinner table. The air hissed and hummed with her furious unspoken reproaches. I toughed it out, counting the days.

I continued to write to Babbie every day and she to me. Reading her letters was unrewarding: Ah well must close now with all my love, that sort of thing. I found that I was straining to recapture that desperate intensity to hold her, keep her, explore her, navigate every inch of her . . . I stared at her huge face in the A4 photograph. Her big calm eyes were tranquil and trusting and empty of challenge and content. I had to call up the image of her sweet rough hands, her broken fingernails, to feel an authentic tremor of desire. The way she said 'fillum', the way she whispered 'that's a mortal sin' . . . the little wet bubbly sound as she caught her breath and licked her upper lip . . . yes, that was better, but still it was an effort. It didn't feel quite real any more.

Not her, then, but my dreams of her image that blossomed a rose in the deeps of my heart. More about me and my yearnings than about her, the person that she was. It was as if I had cried her away.

I didn't like myself much, for feeling like that. It seemed a mean contemptible way to love and I hoped that it was temporary. I told myself that it would be different when I saw her, that it had never been and never would be a cerebral thing, that when I saw her, smelt the sweet baby smell of her head, touched her, heard her soft breath in my ear . . .

I opened the door of my room on the second floor and put my duffle bag down. There she was. Turning from the window with a J-cloth in her hand. A big blonde girl with large expressionless slightly protuberant blue eyes, awkward in her body, her large breasts jutting out of her, smiling at first, then frowning and biting her lip . . .

It had gone. It had all gone. I felt such a shit. Such a fool. Such a self-deluded trifler. What could I say to her? How could I explain?

As it turned out, she had something to confess as well: that she had met another boy over Christmas and she was sorry but she had to tell me that she had been seeing him every day and that she and he were very strong together. But what about all those letters? I asked her. Oh, I know: it's hard to know what to do for the best, she said. I'm so sorry Alan.

I was released. But that didn't change what I felt about me. Shaken.

Where does it go, when it goes? What can we trust? How can I know even now, with Beatrice, my dear one, that I won't one day turn a corner on a stairway, or open a bedroom door, and stare at her baffled, wondering what it was I had seen in her and how it had leaked away?

And what is there left, when it's gone?

I binned the old essays and the textbooks and a bundle of attempts at 'creative writing' but I found I couldn't throw away her letters, and I couldn't throw away her image, either, big and slippery and embarrassing as it is. It's up there now. In its green file.

Beatrice hasn't seen it. Or the letters. She'll be coming in soon. I could show her. I want us to know everything about each other. I could show her. But somehow I don't think I will. Now why is that?

It's up there. In its green file.

It bothers me.

B

The trick is: when you're in the scary place, try to be the scary monster. Even if it's just pretend.

And it was all pretend really. I think I must have been scared shitless all the time. I think we all are now.

That school: it wasn't entirely true that none of the teachers was ever interested in me; there was one who was interested in me for about five minutes, or maybe even longer than that. She may have even thought about me when I wasn't there. You know that thing about 'are other people there when we don't think about them, how can we prove that they really exist?' I used to think a lot about that, only the other way round. I used to wonder if I was really there. Sometimes when I went away from other people, out of the class, say, or into one of the bogs, or just round a corner in a corridor, it would feel as if I had . . . leaked out of the world, passed through some sort of . . . membrane or something, and just sort of stopped existing, until I came round another corner and someone saw me, and sort of . . . called me into being again.

It's a bit fucking scary, feeling like that.

My mother always saw me in those days as part of her, I think, part of her sad life, not a separate person at all . . . what's that stuff called? *Ectoplasm.* As if I was a bit of ectoplasm that had sort of floated off her, right?. . .so that she could be sitting at home being sad, or she could go to other people's houses and sadly clean them, or go to the supermarket and sadly stack the shelves, and meanwhile this ghostly bit of her, this . . .

ectoplasmic manifestation of her loosely known as Beatrice could waft about the streets and lurk in the school bogs waiting for home time before wafting back down the alley and into her sad body again.

Yes, there was this one teacher at that awful school, Miss Townsend her name was, I never found out her first name, it was that sort of place. She was quite young and she taught English, or rather she would have taught English if she could get a hearing. I don't suppose she could have been much good at teaching really; what I liked about her was that she didn't seem quite so hardened as the rest of them. She actually used to read these great long stories I wrote about sensitive young girls with preternatural awareness trapped in brutalising and degrading situations, and she would write comments at the bottom as well. Not the comments I would have wished for, about how brilliantly conceived and movingly written my stories were and what a tragic life-experience they must spring from, and how pleased and excited she had been to elicit them from me. No, she wrote things like 'Quite good, Beatrice, but you have a tendency to over-use parentheses and semicolons.' You would think she would have had an orgasm at the sight of a semicolon even incorrectly used, but that was Miss Townsend for you, that was her way, and seven out of ten was the highest she could bring herself to give anyone for anything; but she was the only teacher I had in the shithole who bothered to write anything on my work; and that made her special for me. (I'm still a bugger for my semicolons. And my parentheses.)

But I couldn't bear to stay in Miss Townsend's classes very long. She would always start off all right, but with something about her that seemed to anticipate trouble before it arrived, and kids would start muttering, and she'd start asking questions she didn't really want to know the answers to, like What are you and Graham Parsons doing under the table, Sean? and What was that you just said under your breath Ganesh? and before long she would be screaming fast and loud over this steady roaring from the kids, and I would feel myself getting this headache like the wound-up spring in the TV advert, and I'd put my hand up and ask to be excused or as often as not just sort of slip out while she was standing there screaming at the kids. No I did not feel sorry for her, she was getting paid for it, why couldn't she do the job right?

Anyway, this one day she came down the girls' toilets and found me there with my smelly little troupe of confederates and she acted as if she was very surprised to see me there, and perhaps she was. She sent Darlene and Jenny and Alma off to their classes, and she told me to sit down on the bench, and she sat down as well and started talking to me in this very low serious voice as if she was a doctor and I had some fatal disease and she was breaking the news that I was about to die in five minutes or something. She asked me what I was doing in the toilets and I said nothing, I just had a headache, that was all, and she went: 'That's not really the truth is it, Beatrice? and I said it was, and then she gave me this really long serious look without saying anything. I started to feel strange, as if I was leaking through the membrane again. I could feel part of myself floating upwards so that I could look down at Miss Townsend and Beatrice on the bench, the fat fair unhappy-looking English teacher and the skinny scruffy shifty-eyed girl . . .

Unreal . . .

She started telling me that I was not like Darlene and Jenny and Alma, that I had gifts which both she and I were well aware of and that I had responsibilities towards those gifts, responsibilities that I was neglecting. It was not just that I was letting her down. It was not just that I was letting the school down. It was not just that I was letting my parents down. (I tried to say that I only had one parent, who could not be any sadder than she was already, but I couldn't make my voice work. I could hear a sort of steady moaning sound begin, and realised that I was making it.) It was myself that I was letting down, Miss Townsend said, in her low quiet voice, as if explaining the pathology of my disease: slowly and surely I was reducing my options and ruining my chances of a happy useful and fulfilling life, and condemning myself to a squalid and brutalised existence which would be all the worse because I had the sensibility to know it for what it was and know that I was capable of something better.

There was some way, I knew, in which her analysis was horribly unfair and skewed, but she was so fucking sure of herself, her pink face nodding, her fat neck flushed, her bulgy blue eyes staring expressionlessly into mine; and I could hear the moaning sound getting louder and stronger, really quite a remarkable sound, not like a little girl giving a series of moans preparatory to bursting into tears, more like a distant aeroplane getting louder and closer, and then Miss Townsend stopped talking and stared at me with her mouth open – I could see her tongue all red and wet – and then my head went fuzzy and I leaked out again, and floated upwards and looked down, and saw myself sort of going mad! I had this mad grin on my face, and the moan had changed to a savage growly sound, and Miss Townsend jerked back and looked very frightened all of a sudden and this seemed to exhilarate me, and I started jumping up and down growling and snarling at her with all great lumps of flob flying out of the corners of my mouth, and I was swinging on the coat hangers and clawing up the thick wire netting thing and crashing down again on the bench and making it bounce and boom, and all the time this horrible loud snarly noise echoing off the bare shiny walls, and Miss Townsend was sort of half leaning half lying against the coat rail, gasping with her mouth open, she didn't seem to be able to move, I think she thought I was going to kill her there, even though I never touched her once.

I was inside myself and outside myself at the same time. It was the first time it had happened. It felt . . . wonderful.

She gave a sort of sobbing cry and ran out, and I kept growling till I couldn't hear her footsteps. Then I stopped. That was strange: I had started it without meaning to, but it seemed I could partly control it. I was trembling all over, and it felt good, like electricity whirling all over my body, all up my legs and down my arms and inside me as well, like coming really, though I didn't know that then.

Another strange thing: you would have sworn that someone like Miss Townsend would have made a big fuss and had me booted out of the school or at the very least sent to the educational psychologist, but she never said anything to anybody, and after that when I asked to be let out of her classes, or even just walked out without asking, she never said a word. What it was, she was terrified of me.

And somewhere at the back of my mind, I thought: now I've done that once, I could do it again.

A

Despite that odd encounter in the strange hot smoky flat in Battersea, despite her occasional absences, that summer in my little gaff in Shepherds Bush was the happiest time I had ever spent, and after a few weeks of it I couldn't imagine how I had coped with living alone and unloved all that time. Just making a mug of tea for her and watching her drink it. Just watching her, you know, just . . . seeing her.

We didn't always make love as soon as she got in from work, but she would nearly always start taking her clothes off as she was coming through the door, press herself against me, always hot, her breath warm on my face, her eyes shining. I was so happy that she was happy to see me.

She would sit on the sofa under the little letterbox window, the sky behind her with the swifts wheeling about, wearing perhaps one white sock, one knee bent, the other over the arm of the sofa, both hands round the blue striped mug, sipping from it with a serious, earnest expression on her face as if drinking her tea was an important task on which both our lives depended. I could never stop myself smiling, watching her drink her tea, and she would catch me watching her and not being able to stop myself smiling:
    'What?'
    'Nothing.'
    '*What?*'
    'Nothing. You, that's all.'
    'You think I'm fucking mental, don't you?'
    'No.'
    'Well you better watch out then cos I fucking am.'

'No, really?'
'Yeah, really. Mental, me. So fucking watch it.'
'I fucking am, I assure you.'
'Yeah, you fucking better. Fucking fuckfaced fuck.'

Our brilliant conversations. I think maybe part of what we were doing that summer was having the childhoods neither of us, in our different ways, had quite managed to have, properly, at the proper time.

Sometimes she would make a mug of tea for me, and I used to find that ridiculously touching, because it had been so long since anyone had done anything like that for me.

We didn't have any friends. Just each other. Well, that's true about me; I'm not quite sure about her. There were her occasional absences, the ones that she didn't explain, and I understood I should not ask about. And her toehold in the flat in Battersea. I think she sometimes had a drink after work with one or two of the 'girlies' from the office. And I think she saw the guys from the gym now and then, Damon and Mick. She mentioned them now and then. She didn't suggest I should meet them, the girlies or the boys, and that was fine with me, because I wasn't really interested in meeting them. I didn't want anyone except her, and when I was with her I found it irritating and unnecessary for either of us to waste any time talking to anyone else. That is not jealousy. That is love. Loving the other person so much that anyone else is a waste of time. That's how I feel, anyway. I don't expect everyone else to feel the same. But the way I see it, if you love one person enough, you don't need friends.

Though come to think of it, I didn't have any friends in the time before I met her, either.

Nothing wrong with that. I was quite happy. I was waiting, that was all. Waiting for Beatrice.

That summer it felt like being drunk all the time, at first. Being drunk on love, drunk on intimacy. Once we had defeated Giant Unfuck, we were desperate to show ourselves to each other in every way we could think of, nothing barred in our innocence.

All the games everyone else seems to have played in their childhood: watching each other piss and shit and masturbate, tasting each other's tastes, tying each other up, exploring each other like secret gardens, sniffing each other all over and grooming each other like monkeys, talking, talking, telling each other stories about ourselves . . .

She would lie, she still does, on the sofa under the window, drinking beer and eating nuts, with the middle finger of her free hand buried up to the second joint in her vagina, humming to herself, smiling her needy smile if I looked over at her.

'What?'
  'Praise me.'
  'What shall I praise?'
  'Praise my cunt.'
  'Your cunt is brilliant and beautiful.'

Pause.

'It's all for you.'

I felt that it was: she was happy to be wholly known in that precise and physical way, she revelled in it, she more or less insisted on it. She was, is, recklessly ungrudging with herself, knowingly risking satiation, weariness, even disgust, wanting to take that risk, wanting, always, to push to the limit.

She had nothing to fear from me in that way. I was intoxicated with her. I am intoxicated with her. I am hooked on her.

And despite all that, I knew there was something more, something she held back, something she couldn't tell me, things about her I might never know.

That evening when she 'borrowed' the cars was nothing: I was shocked a bit, and scared, a bit, but afterwards I thought she was right. It was, as she said, a game. Nothing to be worried about.

There was something else, though. Something more.

B

My dear one was still an anxious lover in a lot of ways. He found it very hard to believe that I could really fancy him; he thought his face was awful: a manky carapace, he said, scarred with old acne wounds. But that was bollocks really, you could hardly see a mark on him; and anyway, that's not the point. He has the sort of face that starts to look beautiful after a while, sort of a *private* beauty apparent only to fantastically discriminating tarts like me, the sort of beauty that needs to be seen through the eyes of love, the drugged and blurry gaze of satisfied desire. Your average girly might not go for him.

But I would. I do.

Can't get enough of his straight gaze, those dark grey eyes looking right into me, so deep and fond, so sure that I am the one, that I am the one he wants.

To live in his gaze is like being cradled in the arms of a strong private daddy who will never go away.

His mouth is the other thing I can't get enough of, so straight and prim till he smiles and then it suddenly looks quite different, curvy and warm and even slightly girly in a strange way. His dear mouth smiling at me. His mouth on my neck, his lips nuzzling my ear. His mouth on my cunt. When I think of his mouth on my cunt I go all shivery.

So why am I such a mad fuck? Where do they come from, these urges to ruin it all by running off and fucking crazy criminals and degenerate losers, and doing other stupid things, some of which carry the more than theoretical risk of long custodial sentences?

Fuck knows.

Fucknose.

I can't help thinking about Paul sometimes. That's OK, nothing wrong with that. It's wanting to go round to see him I should break the habit of. No, wanting's all right, it's actually going there that I should leave out. Well nothing wrong with going round there in itself for old time's sake, that's only friendly, if I could just leave it at that, no problem. Just go round there and have a quiet chat about old times and not have anything to drink and not do any drugs. That would be fine, no problem. But then again, it's no big deal to get slightly smashed once in a blue moon, it's very relaxing to have a few drinks or do some drugs on a strictly occasional and recreational basis, and that's all it is after all, very occasional and strictly recreational. No, it's not really them in themselves, the drink and the drugs, it's the kind of stuff I find myself wanting to do when I've had some. Yeah, all right then, it's not so much the kind of stuff I find myself *wanting* to do, it's *doing* it.

It'll wear off, though, all that, won't it? It's quite new to me, this being good, and it's lovely, it's what I want, I'm changing my life and giving it shape and meaning. Alan is all I want, the rest of it is just . . . nostalgia. And fuck, it's not as if I'm at it all the time, or even very often . . . it's just that now and then . . . ah, shit . . . it's just that being good feels like being suffocated.

Our tutor down the Institute read us this story by Edgar Allan Poe. (Poe and Dostoevsky were his favourite writers, he said, and a haunted-looking fuck he was too.) 'The Imp of the Perverse' it was called, about this young man who commits a perfect murder just for the hell of it, just on a warped whim, just *because* it's such a crazy thing to do. So he kills this kind old man who has befriended him. And then finds himself thinking he's committed such a perfect crime no one could possibly know — unless he confesses! And the moment he thinks of this he gets this perverse urge to confess, and he fights against it and fights against it, and then finishes up going out into the street and yelling over and over again: 'It was I! I am the guilty one! I did it! I killed the old man!'

Prat.

But all the same, I know about that imp, the Imp of the Perverse. I know him well, his name is Fucknose.

Paul is a sweet manipulative bastard, who knows very well how to tug at heartstrings not to mention girlies' undergarments. He can hardly get it up at all these days, what with all the stuff he smokes and swallows and otherwise introduces into his pale and spectral bod, but he has always had such a tender touch, like a dream doctor, you feel yourself melting.

'I never believed anyone would love me for myself, Benny,' he said to me once. 'That's my secret. I always had to try harder than the other guy. I'm not a natural. It's pure technique, darling. Women are drawn to my weakness, and then enthralled by my expertise.'

And then they find out his real secret: he doesn't give a fuck for anyone. But he *is* brilliant at it, no doubt about that, and he can be good fun too, slightly cruel fun sometimes, and I love him still when he gets in a singing mood and sings me all his old songs, all his old Fred Astaire repertoire. Let's Take Our Clothes Off And Dance, all that . . . we did use to take our clothes off and dance, too, he would put on all these dance records and I would leap about like a mad fuck. Paul could do proper ballroom dancing with all the twirls and fancy bits with the lovely straight back surging and nimble toes twinkling away below; he would teach me to do it too, not very successfully because we were usually pissed senseless by the time we got started on the dancing, and we'd fall over quite a bit and find mysterious bruises a few days later. The slow ones were best: he would hold me lightly against his cool thin body and make me sense where he wanted me to go, and for moments together I would feel blessed by his gift, and then we'd stagger and lose it. 'My fault, darling. Wrecked, wrecked, a wrecked talent, and to think what once was there. Benny, I'm sorry, come on dad's feet, I'll make it up to you.' And he'd hold me tighter and lift me so that I was standing with my bare feet on his feet, and we'd dance like a little girl dancing with her daddy. He did let me call him dad and daddy sometimes, when we fucked, too, sometimes, though I think he preferred to be Uncle Paul.

He takes one of my hands in both of his and sings three lines of his favourite song in his rusty sixty-a-day voice:
    The way you hold your knife
    The way we danced till three
    The way you changed my life . . .

The key he sings it in, the word 'life' is quite a high note so that his voice sounds a little strained . . . sometimes he just whispers 'life' instead of singing it. He never sings the last line. He always turns away and talks about something else, or lights a cigarette or something. Crafty sod.

He is jealous of Alan, of course, but he has never spoken a word about him. They've only met each other that one time, when he tried to piss about with Alan. He's never referred to that. I know what it is; he doesn't want Alan to be real, just as Alan doesn't want him to be real. They're so different, but in that way they're just the same. And they both tend to think before they speak, not like me. I say things and I don't know what I've said – I understand what I've said after I've said it, if then, not before. Like one time I said something when Paul was stroking me – I was lying on the dusty carpet in a patch of sunlight, all sprawled out and stark bollock naked, and Paul was sitting by my side in one of his brilliant soft white cotton shirts, drinking a glass of white wine and stroking me softly with his free hand . . . he's so precise and elegant, Paul, all his little movements, every detail right, and so fucked up inside, it makes you want to cry . . . and I was looking at his elegant thin fingers holding the wine glass so lightly, so safely, and feeling the fingers of his other hand stroking me so softly and patiently, as if he had hours and hours to spare and nothing whatsoever to do but what he was doing for as long as I wanted it, his sweet clever fingers utterly at my disposal. The sun was shining through his other hand, the hand that held the wine glass. I could see the red of his blood through his skin, and a little glitter on the soft light hair on his fingers, and all the time his other hand stroking me slowly. All I said was: 'Lovely little hands' but I felt him hesitate for half a second before he went on slowly stroking, and

I thought oh dear, I never used to say 'little' before, I just used to say 'lovely hands' and I knew that in that half second Paul was seeing Alan's strong hands with their long thick fingers. Paul never missed anything like that.

But he never said anything.

What he did say, that time, Paul, was about something quite different and worried me a bit. We were sitting on the sofa by then having a cup of tea. I asked him if he was all right now after that other night when the rough men had come round and bent his piano and everything.

'Yes,' he said, and then, after a pause, 'Well, yes and no.'

He hadn't been hurt too badly. One of them had kicked him in the back a couple of times, which had left him with an enormous purple and yellow bruise about six inches across and a dry cough which worried me although it didn't seem to bother him.

'I'm afraid I laughed at them a bit, and they felt they had to do something to make me take them seriously,' he said. 'They almost apologised, said they'd really only come round to have a word with me, pass on the message as it were.'
    'What message?' I said.
    'Oh, the usual dreary thing about money. Don't worry, Benny, it's all very boring and everything's fine, I've got it covered. Honestly, money. The fuss people make. Anyway I told the chaps not to be so boring about it, and that of course I'd get them some fucking money if they were so fucking desperate for it, and there was no need to be uncivilised, I just simply hadn't realised there was all this desperate hurry.'

He must have known how that would aggravate them.

'What are you going to do?' I said.
    'I'll just take a bigger suitcase on my holidays,' he said. 'Just till this little hiccup's over. It's easy, actually, nothing to worry about, the chaps are always on at me to have a bigger slice, I've always resisted before . . . well it's not my thing, it's just a

hobby really, I don't want people thinking I'm a bagman . . . you wouldn't like to come along, just for the hell of it?'

'No,' I said.

'Just for old time's sake?'

'*No.*'

'Lots of money. Don't you like money any more, Benny?'

'I never did, all that much.'

'What is it, Benny?'

'I just don't do that any more.'

'You do *this.*'

I didn't answer, and he didn't press it. I was lying across his lap with just his cashmere sweater on at the time, his warm fingers curled into my vagina.

'The thing is,' he said after a while, 'I'm not sure there's anyone else I can trust.'

'I'm sorry, Paul,' I said. 'I hate fetching and carrying, it's all just sitting still and feeling anxious, nothing's up to you, it's all up to the other people, it just makes my tummy ache, all right?'

'Oh, Benny,' he said. 'I don't want to make your tummy ache.'

'And anyway I'm straight now.'

'Benny darling,' he said. 'I won't say another word. Everything's fine, I just thought you might fancy a little trip, that's all. We used to have fun on trips; I thought we did. I miss you, Benny. That's all. There's nothing to *worry* about.'

He was worried, though.

'How much do you owe them?' I asked him.

'Hardly anything really, that's the silly thing, just a couple of grand.'

'Come on, Paul,' I said.

'Well,' he said. 'Less than ten, certainly.'

'Why don't you do a film treatment or a rewrite job? Desmond could wangle you ten on signature, easy.'

'Please, Benny,' he said in this pained way. 'I'm not prostituting my gifts just to pay a fucking drug dealer.'

Paul, I wanted to say to him, you *are* a fucking drug dealer.

'Those chaps,' he said. 'They said something about hoping it wouldn't be necessary to bring down David Smith . . . I've heard that phrase before. Is it a code, d'you think, or are they talking about an actual person?'

'Actual person,' I said. 'You wouldn't like him.'

I was shocked to hear his name had been mentioned. David Smith. Fucking hell. Either they were very angry with Paul, or there was more than ten grand in it. If David Smith is looking for you, you are really in the shit. David Smith is a specialist, he comes from Dundee, people send for him. He's an excessive man, a gruesome man. I saw him once, in a pub near Euston station, he was pointed out to me. He wasn't very big, but there was something . . . it was as if he had a kind of force field around him. He was with three other men, they were all talking and he was just sitting there waiting for the talking to be over. He sat with his hands very still, one hand folded over the other hand. The backs of his hands were covered with this reddish brown hair, and he had very thick fingers. He must have noticed me staring, and he looked over at me, just for a second or two. It was frightening.

God, I am so glad I am out of that world and being good now, what I was doing was just kids' games really. Kids' games. If you stay in that world and progress in the career structure, eventually you reach a point where you get to meet people like David Smith socially and professionally on a regular basis. And then you are really fucked, because it's too late to get out.

Paul didn't seem to know anything about him. He asked me what he should do. He asked me whether he should try to get any protection, whether I had any friends who might be able to help. I said no. He asked me whether I might be able to help him myself, at a pinch, and I said no, he didn't realise what he was asking for. He said ah, Benny, people used to be frightened of *you* in the days when we first met. I said they were just kids on the block. We were all just kids on the block once, Benny, he said, even this dreadful fellow Smith, it stands to reason. We were all sweet little babies once, Benny, sucking on our mother's breasts while they cradled us in their arms and dreamed dreams of our future success and happiness, even David Smith, Benny.

I told him that he shouldn't try to protect himself against David Smith or even run away from him. He should be very polite and humble to David Smith and give David Smith exactly what he asked for, and try very hard to do nothing to annoy him. And if David Smith decided to give him a smack there would be nothing Paul or anyone else could do about it.

Well, I was angry with the stupid fuck. And anyway, it's true. There isn't really anything you can do. Well, there's one thing, but I don't think Paul's game for that.

He asked me what giving somebody a smack really meant. I told him it meant killing someone. He went very quiet for a while.

'How's your piano?' I asked him. 'Is it completely fucked?'
    'Well, no,' he said. 'Not completely. Actually,' he said, 'parts of it are excellent.'

A

I've started going to the gym again, pushing myself hard. I'm not sure why I'm doing this. I find myself wanting to do repeated fast circuits with medium weights, increasing my strength and speed, scurrying round the gym like a rat in a cage, irritating the bodybuilders with their big leather bodybelts and their little rinky-dinky gloves. They turn their bovine gaze away from their reflections in the mirror as I strut past them, and stare at me mildly before resuming their sloth-like rituals.

I seem to be preparing myself for something, but I don't know what it is.

When I was about four I had a brief period of being a sort of genius. I was slow learning to read, but I had an affinity with numbers. I liked the patterns that they made and I seemed to be able to understand the way they related to each other without having to think about it. I liked to think about very large numbers. I think that in some odd way I was consoled by the idea of very large numbers. I was pleased that it was 1970, and even more pleased to hear about all the years that stretched backwards before the birth of Jesus, millions and millions of them. I could say that I felt buoyed up by them, all the years that had been lived, but really the main thing was that I just liked thinking about big numbers and saying them to myself. I had a five-year calendar that I liked to look at. Just by glancing at it I could see the patterns in it, and see what the patterns would be in the years before it started and the years after it started, and how surely I could predict what day of the week my birthday would be on in any year, when I was ten, twenty, ninety-nine, a thousand years old.

When my parents noticed my ability they were pleased and excited, and no doubt felt in some way vindicated, for they had (my father told me later) been rather disappointed in me till then. Being so gifted themselves, and having already produced one boy genius in the form of my brother Nick. I became, briefly, a celebrity amongst their friends and colleagues, who would gather round and applaud while I told them the days of their birthdays, this year, next year, the year in which they were born, and so on. My father subjected me to batteries of tests, and declared me officially a prodigy.

My brother Nick brought his friends home to inspect me, and purported to be proud of me, but I think he felt threatened by my odd little gift, because when his friends had gone home he would tease me until I lost my temper and attacked him in a blind rage. This would give him the excuse to beat me up; which he did, in a calm and rather savagely efficient way. It seemed to be essential that I should attack him first, so that in any inquiry the incident could be attributed to my uncontrollable temper. For a long while I actually believed in my uncontrollable temper. Now I think he invented it. Alan's uncontrollable temper. Alan's fits of blind rage. He used to fancy himself as a boxer when he was a kid, Nick, and when I rushed at him with my arms flailing and my eyes blind with tears, he would hit me quickly and expertly and very hard, body blows mostly, I suppose because they hurt a lot but didn't show.

Why did he want to hurt me so much? It couldn't really have been much to do with me, could it? Who did he really want to hurt? Our father, or our mother? I've often wondered, but I have never asked him. It's not the sort of thing you can ask, is it? He is my brother after all.

His birthday is on September 20th and this year it will be a Sunday. I know I'm right; I don't need to look it up to check. And oh yeah, this is rather pleasing: I've just realised that next Wednesday Nick will have been alive for 12345 days. That's not really a very large number, is it? In a strange way it doesn't seem enough. Only twelve thousand three hundred odd days, that doesn't sound like many days. It is though. He's not going to make it to 54321, anyway. Not unless he lives to be nearly 149 years old.

I used to go on like that the whole time when I was four. No wonder I got up people's noses.

Having a temper, being in a temper: that's fine. So long as it isn't an uncontrollable temper. Being in a controlled temper is very good, like driving a powerful car.

Rage. Raging. Being in a rage. Fine, good, excellent. But not a blind rage.

I'm not four years old any more. I think I'm beginning to get the hang of it.

I work out at the gym and I push myself extra hard on the bike. I put on muscle. My reflexes are getting sharper. I'm thinking of going back to the fencing class. I might take extra classes, private ones.

I seem to be preparing myself for something.

I wanted to take her away from London and I wanted to get away myself. Not just the toehold in Battersea. Not just the guy who lurked there with his white shirts and his broken piano and his creepy contacts. Not just the kids I'd seen her with in the gym either, though them too.

No, I had started to feel differently about the school, because of some stuff that happened there.

It was quite a rough school in its way. People laugh when you talk about tough infants, but in fact they were much more violent than secondary school kids. Some of them had ten or twenty fights a day: it was a compulsion. The playground was a battlefield, and you could see them longing for the order of the classroom. Being bad must be a terrible strain sometimes, I think.

A lot of them felt the need to have a go at me, the little boys mostly. They wanted to see how far they could push me. A lot of them didn't have fathers at home. They were interested in finding out the differences between a man and a lady. I found their aggression rather touching; it was as if they wanted to make me a present of it. But it was difficult to know what to do with it. I often felt tender towards them, their little raw angry faces, and I wanted to cuddle them out of their anger, cuddle them and cradle them the way I sometimes did with Beatrice. One or two of the women teachers used that technique, and I envied them.

Cuddling infants is misconstrued if you're a man.

What I did with the very difficult kids is use Behaviour Modification. Basically what you do is reinforce desired behaviours by rewarding them, and discourage undesired behaviours by ignoring them. The point is that bad kids usually hear only bad things about themselves: they are always getting punished and eventually they get criminalised. With BM they hear only good things about themselves. The only way they can get attention is by being good. They learn about the pleasures, rewards and opportunities of being nice to other people. They modify their behaviour as a result.

Yeah, yeah, it's soulless and mechanical and yeah, yeah, it comes from the States. Heard it. Reduces complex human souls to bundles of behaviour patterns. Heard it, not interested. Because all we can know about other people is their behaviour, patterned or not. What they do. What they do to themselves. What they do to other people. What they do to us. The rest is just fantasy, our fantasy about the other people.
     Naturally we prefer the fantasy.

I certainly do.

I was trying to use Behaviour Modification in a disciplined way with Ricky Sturge. It's appallingly difficult, making yourself ignore all those things that seem to cry out for attention, not to say retribution, and remember to be nice to him for really rather unremarkable things like sitting still for a whole minute without yelling out, or hitting someone, or perpetrating some piece of minor vandalism. Ricky Sturge was a pale, ratty little kid with small greenish eyes: his face was usually blank, but you could sometimes detect fear there, or contempt, and more rarely he smiled a brief creepy smile. I was working on his smile amongst other things, encouraging him to make it bigger and broader, and use it more frequently, not just when someone else was getting hurt or in trouble. It was one of the behaviours I was rewarding, for my own sake as well as his. I thought I might like him better if he gave me a nice smile now and then. And I thought he might like me better. There is a good deal of empirical data indicating that smiling makes people feel happy. Rather than the other way round, I mean.

Well, it made a change from yelling at him all the time which is what everyone else did, because he really was a dreadful kid. Yelled at all day in school and knocked about at home.

But there is a snag in Behaviour Modification: for the teacher in charge of a whole group of children, there are some undesired behaviours that cannot be ignored, and so it proved with Ricky Sturge . . .

Oh fuck fuck *fuck* why am I trying to talk about this in such a cool amused ironic and professional way because I am still upset about it whenever I think about it because I don't understand what happened with Ricky don't understand about me about teaching about man or lady about kids about bad kids about her about Beatrice about her about her about her her her.

Ah fuck it, say it, say what happened, it won't take long.

We'd had quite a good day, me and Ricky. He'd been good right up to afternoon play: I'd found twenty-three occasions to praise him, I'd even won three rather sneaky grudging smiles from him, found myself feeling quite tender towards him, caught myself thinking he's got quite a sweet little ratty face really, all this while keeping the other twenty-seven kids feeling happy and attended to – it's quite a game teaching six-year-olds. Yes, all right: I was feeling pleased with myself.

Then during afternoon playtime it all went wrong. I wasn't there but apparently he started hitting Gurpreet Mojinder's little brother and Gurpreet, a thickset top-knotted seven-year-old chap with an incipient moustache, laid one on Ricky, upon which Ricky kicked Gurpreet 'in the tentacles' as Gurpreet put it, and temporarily disabled him. Judy Purvis, who was out there on duty, dragged them both in and made them stand in the corridor outside Sally's room. While he was standing there, Ricky kicked a hole in the wall. Not a difficult feat in our school, even for a six-year-old. He claimed the hole was there already, or some of it, and I believe him: but the caretaker, who happened to be passing, went into an instant rage when he saw the debris, and did a lot of shouting into Ricky's face, which rather frightened him, I think.

He was a bit pale and shaky when he came back into the classroom and his eyes looked smaller and sharper. I couldn't get him to look at me; his gaze kept darting about. People use the expression 'looking for trouble'. He seemed to be doing that, literally. I asked him if he'd sharpen a few pencils for me. They all liked doing that. I had one of those big old-fashioned important-looking teacher's pencil sharpeners clamped to my table. Very therapeutic. The secret is you turn the handle very slowly, hear the little rustly hiss as curly shavings roll themselves seductively off the ever sharpening point. A simple, pure, totally reliable pleasure.

I let him sharpen four and watched his face soften. He went back to his table with the pencils. The kid next to him, Carlo Bencivenga, picked up one of them, a bright red one, and Ricky instantly snatched it back and stabbed Carlo in the cheek with it. The pencil remained hanging out of Carlo's cheek like some lopsided tribal decoration and we all stared at it for several seconds in an awed way. I remember thinking ridiculously that he looked like a woman with one earring. Then the pencil fell out of his cheek, bounced on the table and skittered on to the floor. Carlo seemed to come to life and snatched up another of the pencils, a bright green one, but by then I was down amongst them. I picked up Ricky and carried him to the empty book corner and plonked him down on the cushions. I said: 'Stay there. Don't move.' I am sure that is all I did. What else would I have done? The kids I teach are capable of terrible violence, but they are all, thank God, comparatively weak, light, and portable. Ricky offered no resistance at all: he seemed stunned by his own actions. I sent Carlo to the secretary who is good with minor lacerations and knowing when to head for Casualty. And that was it, really. We were all very quiet for the rest of the afternoon. I could feel Ricky glaring at me, but as he stayed still, I didn't look his way directly again. My head felt hot, I remember, and my ears were singing. I noticed that my hands were shaking.

At home time I checked with the office. Carlo had been judged severely damaged enough for Casualty. I wrote out a one-page report on the incident, and fucked off home on my bike. The air felt thick and sweet and dirty. Back in the flat I stood under the feeble trickly shower for a long time, thinking of nothing, waiting for Beatrice to come home.

The next morning I was called into June's office. June, the head teacher. June, my boss. Stocky, smiley. Tough as old Docs. Ricky Sturge was there with his mother. His face was marked. His nose had been bleeding. There was dried blood in his ear. There was a red angry lump on his cheekbone with a bruise spreading round it. His mother looked tense and angry. Her fists were clenched and she was breathing loudly through her nose. A big woman, bigger than me. She looked fat but strong. About thirty. I had seen her before but we had never spoken; she had never come to a parents' evening. Ricky wouldn't look up at me. His mother was looking at me as if she thought she could hurt me with her eyes. June looked . . . wary, I thought.

June asked me what had happened the previous afternoon, and I told her.
    'And that's all?'
    'Yes, that's all as far as I know,' I said.
    'Fucking liar,' said Mrs Sturge in a loud strained voice, as if she was anxious to come out clearly on some distant tape recorder.
    'Um, Ricky claims you picked him up and, er, threw him against the wall,' said June.
    'Three times. Slammed him into the wall three times,' said Mrs Sturge. 'Slammed his face into it.' In an odd way, she sounded more satisfied than outraged.

'Is that right, Ricky?' said June.

Ricky nodded, his face still down.

'Look at me, Ricky. Is that right, what your Mum just said?'

Ricky looked up, at June, not at me.

'Yes,' he whispered, and looked down again.

'That's not true,' I said. 'He knows that.'

'Are you calling him a liar? Are you telling me my son would lie to me? Is that what you're telling me?'

Oh, God, I thought.

'He's six years old,' I said. 'They all do – it's no big deal.'

'It is to me,' she said. 'My son would never lie to me. Never!' Pause. 'Because he knows what he'd get if he tried!'

'What would he get?' I asked her. 'His face slammed into a wall?'

My voice was trembling.

'What did you say?' said Ricky's mother dangerously. 'Did you hear what he said?' she asked June.

'Alan, I don't think that remark was really helpful,' said June. 'I think we're all grown up enough to discuss this in a constructive way.'

Despite her words she was treating me like a child. I felt like a child too: weak, light, skittery. Tears pricking at the backs of my eyes.

'He didn't get those injuries in school,' I said. 'Did he?'

Christ, even my voice sounded faintly tearful to me.

'You're quite positive you didn't touch him, Alan?'

'I told you I touched him,' I said. 'I picked him up and carried him over to the book corner. That's all.'

Ricky looked up suddenly.

'You slammed me down,' he said softly.

'Hey,' I said. 'Come on, Ricky. You know that's not true.'

He turned his face away. I knew I was right, but I felt wrong.

'I think he should go on the At Risk list,' I said. 'I think he's being physically abused at home and that's why he's so violent in school.'

I couldn't stop my voice shaking. There was a long pause. No one was looking at anyone else. The little room with its shiny cream walls festooned with kids' work seemed to boom and thrum.

'Alan,' said June eventually, 'would you wait outside for a few moments?'

I went out and sat on the chair outside June's room. Judy Purvis walked past and glanced at me curiously. She didn't smile. I looked away. She doesn't like me, I realised. She never has. Neither does June. I'm good at my job, I help out, so it's difficult for them to say it. They don't have a reason, they can't put their finger on it, but they don't like me.

Well, fuck them. I felt light and feathery, I felt as if I needed something to hold me down, something inside me, some weight in my stomach to hold me down.

Ricky Sturge came out of June's room and walked towards the Year Two area where Alice was covering my kids as well as hers. He didn't look at me. He was walking fast and looking down.

'Ricky,' I said.

He turned. I had called him without thinking what I would say.

'It's OK,' I said. 'Everything will be OK.'

He didn't say anything. After a moment he turned and scuttled off again. Like a rat, like a crab, like a spider, like a ghost, a ghost from my childhood. He's like I used to be, I thought, he's like me.

Then his mother came out. I stood up. She came very close to me and said: 'Look, teacher. You lay one finger on my little boy again, I'll kill you.'

I couldn't believe my ears. Had she really said that?

'Don't try to threaten me,' I said. I was trying to sound cool and contemptuous but it came out high and quavery.

Slowly, thoughtfully almost, as if she had tasted blood, she pushed her face forward so that it was only inches away from mine, and bared her teeth.

'I'll bite your fucking face off, teacher,' she said.

Her breath smelt rank and meaty.

'Come on then,' she said.

I imagined stepping forward hard on to her feet, jerking her head forward, smashing my bony forehead into her thick nose. Taking her wrist, leaning back and using her own weight to swing her round fast off balance to slam into the opposite wall.

'Come on. Try it,' she said. She was breathing fast. Her eyes were cloudy and unfocused. She was excited. She was turned on.

'Try it,' she said. 'Hit me.'

I couldn't move.

'You fucking coward,' she said. 'I know what you are, you're fucking queer, aren't you? You're a fucking pervert.'

'Leave me alone,' I said.

I was feeling frightened, but not of her.

'Fucking nance,' she said.

She wanted me to hit her. She wanted to be hurt.

'Come on then,' she said.

She was whispering now.

I knew that soon I was going to do something terrible.

'Alan.'

It was June, in the doorway.

'Alan, could you come back in, now? I'll be in touch, Mrs Sturge.'

I turned and looked back at Ricky's mother before I went in. She had her arm out straight, pointing at my face, her thick finger like a gun in my face.

'Any time,' she said. 'Any time you like.'

'Any time what?' said June when we were inside with the door closed.

'I don't know,' I said. 'I think she's a bit disturbed.'

'Any time *what*, Alan?'

'Well it sounds ridiculous but I think she meant any time I wanted a fight she was ready for one.'

'You do seem to have ... rubbed her up the wrong way, somehow, don't you?' said June. 'How did that happen, do you think?'

She was smiling at me in a patient, professional way.

'What?' I said. 'I mean, you were there.'

'I wasn't in the classroom when you ... manhandled Ricky, Alan. And I wasn't in the corridor just now. So I'm not at all clear what went on. On either occasion. And I think on the whole it might be better if things stay like that. Don't you?'

'Christ,' I said. 'D'you mean you don't believe me?'

'I told Leanne Sturge I had absolute confidence in you. But I agreed with her that it might be better if Ricky transferred out of your group. So that's what he's going to do. Is that OK with you, Alan?'

'No,' I said. 'We're doing OK, me and Ricky. It's a new mother he needs, not a new teacher.'

She raised her eyebrows at me and her spectacles slid down her nose. She had those little half-moon ones. Part of her Senior Management gear. She had a square-shouldered dark grey chalk-stripe jacket as well, she wore it (subtle mixed message) over the official school charity T-shirt with the two little stick people holding hands – ah, shit, she looked all right, she looked fine, it isn't the clothes, it's the sick dead language that we all have to speak at work, this language it's impossible to tell the truth in, or say how we are feeling, till everything is stained and diseased with lies, the big brown stains spreading over the shiny professional public teeth . . .

'Look, Alan,' she said. 'It happens to all of us sometimes. One of them, or sometimes a particular group of them, really winding you up. I absolutely understand. Absolutely. But when it reaches crisis point, sometimes you have to simply walk away until it simmers down. Until *you* simmer down. Just walk away. OK?'

I was feeling sick. I had to say it though.

'You think I hit him, don't you?'

'Of course not,' she said. But she did. She did. 'I told you, I have absolute confidence in you, Alan. As I have in all my staff.'

After a bit, she moved the subject round to my career: how golden a future lay in front of me, able young men being so rare in primary teaching. What I needed to do was to move around, get experience in different parts of the country, I wasn't doing justice to my talents, I was ripe already for a post of responsibility. If I made the right moves, I should have a school of my own by my early thirties. I couldn't understand at first why she was saying all this, and then it came to me it was a polite way of asking me to get the fuck out of her school please as soon as possible and that if I did my references would be excellent. With perhaps the tiniest hint of my possible propensity for slamming six-year-olds into walls.

All that day, his shy shifty gaze.

I didn't need to ask him. He had told his story to divert his mother's violent rage. It hadn't worked but he had had to stick to it. I didn't blame him for that. I felt tender towards him. He was like me.

You slammed me down, he said. He knew I hadn't. But it had been in me, and he had felt it. He had felt me stopping myself doing it.

In some ways he had no power at all and in other ways he was very powerful. Ricky Sturge. He was to do with violence the way some people are to do with sex. He sensed the violence in you and he drew it out of you. A family talent, it seemed.

All that day, his shy shifty gaze. He wore his scars like military decorations. Spoke to no one.

I rewarded his appropriate behaviours and ignored the rest. He was considerate, and didn't push too far. I let him sharpen pencils and he was content to watch the fat shavings whispering off the scented wood.

I didn't know what to do about him. I didn't know what to do about his mother. I didn't know what to do about myself.

That night it was hot. My little flat under the roof was throbbing with it, as if the house had a headache. I could feel her shifting and tossing, restless by my side, but sleep pulled me down irresistibly; my bones melted into the mattress.

I was struggling with Ricky Sturge's mother in the corridor outside June's room. I was trying to stop her going up the winding stone staircase to the dormitories upstairs where the children slept: she accepted now that Ricky was a little liar and she wanted to beat it out of him she said, beat him until he was as pale and pure as chicken meat she said, beat the bad blood out of him, beat it out of his little chicken breast, she said. I was trying to reason with her, saying don't you see that'll kill him, he'll be dead if you beat the blood out of him, but she wouldn't listen, just kept saying the same thing over and over, beat it out of him, chicken meat, and then not words at all, just a sort of gargling, her mouth was wide open and there was blood in her mouth as if she had bitten her tongue, or her gums were bleeding or something had wounded her mouth. Her flesh looked pale and puffy but her muscles were strong, not soft as I had imagined. She was terribly strong, and she wrenched and twisted and wriggled in my grip, snarling and spitting in my face and trying to turn her head to bite my hands. She was slippery and too strong for me in her purple nylon tracksuit, my fingers were slipping on the material, I couldn't get a purchase on it. I felt that she was going to get away from me and murder the children sleeping upstairs, in the hot dark dormitory under the throbbing roof, murder them in their beds, perhaps eat parts of them, and I started shouting for help, but it was the middle of the night, the school was dark and damp and foggy like a Florida swamp, and I wasn't going to be able to hold her any more. Snarling, she twisted free and started scrambling up the wet stone steps and I grabbed at her, caught her legs and she slipped, pulled, and her tracksuit trousers came down to her knees and her huge pale bottom, a bright tuft of gingery hair sprouting incongruously from the black ravine, loomed into my face as, growling, she struggled on up the stairs in a series of convulsive jerks, like a contestant in some obscene children's sack race. I lost my grip again, she kicked backwards into my face, I lost my footing and tumbled backwards, bumping the back of my head on the wall at the bottom of the stairwell. Somehow I had got soaking wet all over. I was dizzy. I felt unwell and uneasy. Then I realised that the stairway was empty, that she had got away, that she was up there amongst the children, and I pulled myself up and scrambled up the scummy stone steps on my hands and knees.

As I came round the corner into the strange blueish light of the dormitory I could see all the children sitting up in their iron beds watching round-eyed. She was crouching, waiting for me, naked except for her tattered, bloodstained vest. Look, I said to her, maybe we don't have to fight, I don't want to hurt you. She started to laugh this strange gargling laugh, and jumped at me, twisting her head so that she could get her face to the side of the neck to bite my throat out. She was terribly strong. I felt her cheekbone bumping along my jaw, felt her sharp teeth grazing my throat, then I jerked my head back, held her face steady for a second, my hands twisted in her hair, and I banged my forehead down on her nose. I started to sob. Not for myself; because of what I had done. It had all gone wrong. I had just wanted to stop her hurting the children and now I was killing her. She jerked one hand free and got two fingers into one of my eye sockets, the left one, trying to pop my left eyeball out. Just as I felt her fingers scooping and cupping round it, I butted her again, and she gasped and let go. My face was wet and sticky. I got behind her, forced her down, banged her face into the stone floor. And again. There was wetness in the sound now, a sort of plashing. I was crying. It had all gone wrong. It had all gone wrong.

She had stopped struggling now. I lay on her limply, my chest to her back. She was breathing slowly. I hadn't killed her, but she had stopped trying to kill me. Her body was warm. Her breathing was steady and strong. I felt immensely relieved. Perhaps I had not damaged her irrevocably after all.

With an immense effort I heaved her over. She didn't resist, but her body seemed dauntingly heavy. Whale-heavy, heavy as a sack of wet sand. But finally I managed to turn her and she flopped over on to her back. Her eyes were closed. Her nose was spread across her face. Her mouth was swollen and glistening with blood, her lips open. Her fat red tongue. I looked down, and her cunt was wide open too, red, wet, pulsing like a heart, huge as a cave. She opened her eyes and reached for my prick and for a split second I knew who she really was, then it went away as she drew me down and I panicked then because I knew that if she got my whole face in her mouth I would drown.

It was light outside. I was soaked with sweat. My head was hammering. I reached for Beatrice but she wasn't there. My first confused thought was that I had done something dreadful to her. I had murdered her, that was it, I had murdered her because I feared I couldn't hold her, I had murdered her and hidden her body somewhere and then forgotten all about it. Was that it? I

138

felt guilty of something but I didn't know what. Perhaps I had committed some awful deed and she knew about it, Beatrice knew about it, my crime, she had divined it by osmosis because it was a crime of the heart, I had sweated my involuntary confession into her in the night, the knowledge had passed from my skin into hers, and the knowledge had been so terrible that she had been unable to bear it, she had been unable to bear going on living with me, and she had left me. Yes, that was it.

Those dark fantasies we have on the edge of sleep and waking. Are they there to tell us the truth about ourselves, or are they just brain-waste, random scrambled bits of shredded dream that have slipped out of the filing system? I told myself my dark sick feeling was just a leftover, a phantom way of worrying about Ricky, that everything was safe and right and that my dear one loved me, but it didn't work. I was coming out of sleep now, hauling myself laboriously out of it like a man scrambling up out of a dark well. My right arm was numb where I had been lying on it. I couldn't make a fist. I looked at the clock. It said 0540. Beatrice wasn't there. I listened. The flat was terribly quiet. Outside, a bird had started to sing.

She had left me.

I got up and walked stiffly into the front room.

She was sitting on the sofa, naked, her chin on her knees, hugging her legs, staring into space.

'Hello,' I said. 'I missed you. I thought you'd gone away.'
    'No,' she said. 'Couldn't sleep, that's all.'
    'I had such awful dreams,' I said.
    I sat down by her. I still couldn't quite believe she was there.
    I said: 'At first when I woke up I thought I'd killed you – isn't that weird?'
    'No,' she said. 'I think you'd like to sometimes.'
    I touched the skin on her round knee. It felt thin, like silk over the muscle, a blueish translucency under the brown. I loved her so much it made me catch my breath; how could I want to kill her?

She turned and looked at me hard. She wasn't smiling.

'I give you a hard time, don't I?' she said.

'No,' I said. 'Not really. I don't like it when you're not with me. I worry I'm going to lose you.'

'Be the other way round,' she said. 'Nothing lasts, with me. You think I'm lovely but eventually you'll be disgusted with me.'

I laughed.

'Don't laugh at me,' she said. 'It's true.'

'It's not,' I said. 'Everything is going to be OK.'

I wish I could stop saying that.

'So what were these dreams?'

'I was fighting this woman,' I said. 'And I thought I'd killed her.'

'Was it me?' she said.

'No, it was a woman called Mrs Sturge. Did I tell you about Ricky Sturge? His mother.'

'But it was me really.'

'No, it was her. She wasn't anything like you. She had a shiny purple tracksuit and a huge white arse and coarse ginger pubic hair.'

'You fucked her, didn't you?'

'No, I didn't. I mashed her face in, I was crying, I was sorry for her, her poor face, but it didn't stop me doing it. I didn't stop until I thought I'd killed her. It was a hell of a relief when I found I hadn't. She didn't look too bad really. Her nose was squashed and her mouth was . . . she didn't seem to be irreparably damaged.'

'What sort of shape was her cunt in?'

'What?'

'You heard.'

'It seemed to be all right,' I said, evasively. Somehow I didn't feel like going into detail about huge hot wet red caves.

'So you thought you might as well fuck her after all.'

'Look,' I said. 'It was a dream, for God's sake.'

'You don't love me any more,' she said. 'You sleep with me and dream about other women. This is it. This is the start of the bad times.'

She turned her face to me. She looked utterly miserable. I

thought, she depends on me. She depends on me. I felt lovely in that moment, like a wise elder brother.

'Hey,' I said. 'This is all shit, all this stuff about other women, you know it is. You know I only love you, you know I only want you. You have nothing to fear. No one else will do, there is no substitute, I thought I'd made that clear.'

'No other cunt will do?'

'No other cunt will do.'

I put my hand over it and she shifted her position to accommodate me.

'Look,' I said. Can I ask you something?'

'All right,' she said.

I was beginning to focus my anxieties: it was the stuff at school I was really worried about, I thought, and she could help me with it.

'Well . . . when you were having your, your criminal career, you must have, well, hurt people sometimes. Done their faces in, as they say. For example. Yes?'

She didn't say anything.

'I was wondering, did it worry you . . . sort of wanting to hurt them, and then actually hurting them, and then when you saw what you'd done, didn't it . . . I mean wasn't it a bit upsetting? – I mean their poor faces all mashed up and that?'

'I don't want to talk about that,' she said.

'It's not just idle curiosity. I sort of need to know. I need to know what makes people want to do that stuff.'

'Well, I don't want to talk about it, all right? It's all over, all that, I've told you.'

'You like talking about some bits of it,' I said. 'You like to shock me about the cars and the robbing, you love all that B. Monkey read my name stuff. If that's all right to talk about, why not this?'

'Don't want to. Don't want to think about it. It's part of why I gave it up. Will you move your hand away now please?'

I moved my hand.

'Thank you.'

She put her chin on her knees and stared ahead again for some seconds.

'We never set out to hurt anyone,' she said. 'It just happened sometimes. What are you trying to do, make me feel shitty about myself?'

'Why did you do any of it?' I asked her.

I couldn't help it. I wanted to know all about her but more than that I wanted to know all about me; I had all this stuff inside me that had never come out since the days when I had launched myself screaming with rage and frustration into my big brother's quick accurate fists, and she had been through it all and come out the other side or so she said, done and seen in life what I had only done and seen in dreams or watched on flickering screens. And yes, all right: I wanted to make her feel shitty.

'Fuck knows,' she said. 'Imp of the Perverse.'

'What?'

'Imp of the Perverse,' she said. 'Fucknose his name.' She gave a little creepy grin. 'D'you like it?' Then she said: 'Please don't ask me any more now, Alan.'

I didn't. We sat there side by side. It was a quarter to six in the morning. After a while she began to talk again. She told me she was worried about herself. She told me that she did things she didn't want to do, that she did them *because* she didn't want to do them. Because of Fucknose, the Imp of the Perverse. She said I shouldn't ask her why: she'd only say because. She said I shouldn't ask her what the things were in case she told me. She said she still did some of those things but not so many, she was getting better now because of me, I was her dear one and her best hope. She asked if we could get back into bed and hold each other.

Ah, B. Monkey. Making love to her that morning was like coming back from the dead.

Her sweet smile like a little sister as she sucked her own juices from my four fingers curled into her mouth. Her little high cries.

Beatrice Monkey.

*

I rode to school that day a prince of men. Black taxis deferred to me and battered Transits waved me on. I smiled at Ricky Sturge with what I think was genuine affection, and he smiled back at me.

I got on the phone and shopped his mother to the Social Services.

And then I went to June and handed in my resignation.

B

Went to work dirty that day. Liked to do that sometimes. Liked to go to school dirty too when I was little, when my mother was too preoccupied or depressed to make me wash. Pull off the frowsty nightie, straight into the clothes that were warming on the wire fireguard, off to school hugging all my cosy night smells inside my clothes, my private secrets.

And I had got back into it that summer with my dear one, not every day of course, just sometimes. Roll out of bed still kissing him and pull on last night's richly evocative knickers and yesterday's lived-in clothes. Resist the urge to wash, even a lick and a promise. No deodorant. Streak of lipstick, drag the comb through six times max, and out clipclopping in my little black courts along the smart end of Elgin with the houses looking in permanent intensive care, all life-supports and bridgework, with the big boys on the scaffolding gripping their crotches and howling for me like banshees, little knowing that my dear one's spunk was even now oozing slow and stately as volcanic lava down my inner thigh. Strange what a lovely feeling that is when you're crazy about him, and how tedious and slimy and just plain fucking nasty leaking come is when you're going off your lover even just a tiny little bit.

Sitting at my desk and talking on the telephone, smelling of him, smelling of us, all the time massaging the insatiable egos of the wankers whose calls Desmond wasn't returning that day – the few he really rated went straight through to him on his super-double-secret direct line – with one finger under my nose, inhaling the mingled fragrance of my boyfriend's come, my own vagina, and a chocolate digestive biscuit donated by my employer, I was as happy as I think I've ever been. Because I was crazy about him, and I knew I had lucked out this time: the first one I had ever loved who wasn't mad, or evil, or untrustworthy, or insensitive, or fucked up with drugs, or married, or a shit. And he was mad for me too, desperate, adored me. All I had to do was love him back, stay faithful, and keep off the criminal pursuits and I was headed for a long and happy life. And to do these things would be easy, because I was a girl in love.

So how was it that I found myself making a little space between wankers so that I could call Damon and fix a meet that very evening when I knew the places it would lead me?

Fuck knows.

Fucknose.

Armed robbery is a doddle if you follow a few simple rules. The odds in your favour are enormous. The trouble is, most armed robberies are committed by criminals, and criminals hate following simple rules. They are often mad fucks as well. Most of them are stupid. Most of them are prone to grassing on their mates. Many armed robbers are well known to the police as such. Obviously those ones are going to get arrested a lot. So the rules are: never work with anyone who's been done for it, and never work with grassers, thickies, mad fucks or dope fiends. Or wanks who are going to bottle out on you, obviously.

The work itself is simple: you go in there looking dead fierce, frighten the shit out them and take their money or whatever it is you have come for. It's so easy you wonder how anyone gets caught.

Because they're thickies, mad fucks, grassers, wanks and dope fiends, that's why.

He was sitting with Damon in the Albany when I came in. John Hart his name was and he looked faintly Irish, black hair and dark blue eyes, rosy lips like a girl's. He didn't look frightfully clever. But big. Usefully big. Ridiculously big. Six three at least, with these great big red Irish hands, and thick wrists sticking out of his blue jacket, great thick things like blocks of wood, and all this thick wiry black hair coming out of his sleeves like a Guy Fawkes with his stuffing coming loose. He had his own one-man business he said, supplying and laying carpets.

'That must be interesting,' I said politely, thinking how boring and horrible it must be, on your knees all day with your nose at the level of other people's boots.

'Well, now, it is and it isn't,' he said. 'But that's work for you. Do you have a job yourself?'

I told him I was a tattooist and Damon started giggling. I thought ah fuck, let's have a bit of fun then, and I ordered a large gin and tonic.

I wanted it to be Mick not him, I love Mick, we were all in the unit together, Mick and me and Damon and Bruno, deep friends, die for each other, but Mick was in Belfast, had been for six months, and this John Hart had apparently done a couple with Damon and Mick that had gone quite well. You could see he was very impressed and intrigued to be meeting me. He'd heard of me. He'd read my name.

'I didn't think you'd be such a little thing,' he said winningly. I thought leave off, I wouldn't shag you if you were the last man on earth. What am I doing sitting here talking to a plank like you?

I knew what I should do: drink up, put the glass down, stand up, walk out and go home to my boyfriend. Maybe pick up a vid and a bottle of wine on the way. I don't need to spend my time with mad fucks and losers. I have too much to lose myself now. All I have to do is get up, say goodbye, walk out and everything will be fine.

We arranged it for the next day, in my lunch hour.

I woke very early that morning. Watched Alan sleeping for a while. He'd been fine the night before, asked me nothing, just so pleased to see me, I love the way he trusts me and accepts me, why the fuck do I get up to all this nonsense? Stroked his sleeping chest. Held his soft dick. Its little blind face, fast asleep.

At half past twelve I walked out of the office and round the corner where Damon was waiting in a BMW he'd popped not five minutes earlier in Portland Road. He was in a nice black suit and had his hair tied back. I sat in the back. I was wearing a smart little black dress Paul had bought me in New York once, and I had a Fenwick's carrier bag with some things in it. We picked John Hart up on Holland Park Avenue, he was not looking bad at all, considering, in a dark suit with a buttonhole and a polka-dot bow-tie, though he had spoilt it all by carrying his gun in a Head sports bag that might as well have had SWAG written on it. He looked a bit white around the gills I thought, but even bigger than he had looked last night. If he could be fierce as well as big he'd be lovely; nobody would think of having a go at him.

We were all a bit quiet on the way down to Bond Street. Oh yes we all know how easy it is, or should be, but look at all the fuck ups that can happen, the fucking traffic gets more desperate day by day, that's what I was worrying about most, the traffic and this new fuck Hart, whether he was up to it, whether he'd stand up, how much I'd rather it was me and Mick and Damon, even though we were all a bit short in stature for your classic armed robbery. But mostly I was feeling the old buzz surging and bouncing round my body up and down my strong young arms and legs ho ho you fuckers Beatrice Monkey on the rob today, do what I say and stay out of my way because I am a mad fuck baby don't care what I do you better believe it.

Lovely, lovely when the sick nerves go and everything goes icy cool and almost slow motion. I could tell Damon was feeling good too as we swung round the corner nice and slow, my sweet gentle driver stroking the wheel around. He was in the front like our chauffeur, in his black suit with the hair tied back, so handsome. I got the hats out of the Fenwick's bag, big black wide-brimmed one for me, brown Christies felt for him. Put on my dark glasses and gloves. Held out my hand for Hart's piece and put it in the Fenwick's bag. He was still looking a bit pale I thought. Damon stopped on the double yellow outside the shop, switched on the hazard flashers and released the bonnet catch.

'Come on, killer,' I said to Hart, and we walked into the shop arm in arm. There were just two customers, an old guy with a belly and his girlfriend. The manager. Two assistants, both men, all in the black jacket grey waistcoat crap. We walked straight up to the manager and I had the piece out of the Fenwick's bag and into Hart's hand one second before the guy looked up.

'This is a robbery,' said Hart in this hoarse wheezy voice. He cleared his throat. 'Get down on the floor, face down.'
  What was the matter with him? He seemed to have lost his voice. He was swaying a bit. He grabbed on to the counter with his left hand. Shit, I thought, he's going to faint.
  'I beg your pardon, sir?' said the manager. He wasn't doing it right either. He didn't seem to notice he had a gun pointing at his belly. Jesus.

I took the tyre lever out of my Fenwick's bag.
  'Fucking robbery, man!' I yelled as loud and deep as I could. 'Get on the fucking floor face down or you are dead! All of you, fuck it! Now!'
  They were still all standing there staring at us. About half an hour seemed to go by, I dare say it was only half a second, then I smashed the glass counter, right by the manager's hand, the glass was shooting everywhere, I heard him gasp, and Fatty's girlfriend gave a little girly scream, and then I went down the whole row of glass cases, giving them stick, showing the punters a bit of style and badness, bang crash bang crash bang crash bang, then I said 'Right then you fuckers who's first?' and to my great relief they all lay down on the floor.

A bell started ringing and Hart said 'Oh, Jesus!' in this little high voice. We had talked it all over last night, how the manager would bravely set the alarm off and that from then on we had four minutes clear before the fastest possible police response, and all we needed was forty-five seconds, because we weren't bothering with the safe, just clearing out the rings and pendants on display. We had been through it all a million times and still the wank was panicking.

'Just hold the gun, killer,' I said. I was feeling fine, now they all had their faces in the carpet. Neat, cool, and strong. I had slowed the world down. I walked down the counter emptying the cases into the Fenwick's bag. I could hear the fat old boy grunting and wheezing. His breathing didn't sound too good. Too much rich food no doubt and teenage poontang. 'Everything's fine, folks,' I said. 'You're being very good. We'll just be two minutes now. You can count up to a hundred and twenty slowly, then get up very slowly. Don't count too fast, or you'll get up too soon and my friend will shoot you.' Luckily they couldn't see my friend from where they lay.

Outside I could see Damon putting the bonnet down. People were going past on the pavement. No one seemed to be looking in. Inside, the staff and the customers were lying still. I took the gun off Hart. For a second I had this mad impulse to spray a few shots round, do a little damage, go a little crazy. Hart read it, somehow. I saw the fear in his eyes and he swayed again and his eyes went up, and I thought he's fainting again, fucking fine robber *he* turned out to be. I put the gun in the Fenwick's bag with the jewellery and the tyre lever. Then I took his arm and we walked out of the shop.

Hart was weak at the knees. He could hardly walk. His face was yellowy white and covered with great big beads of sweat. But nobody took much notice of us, even with the alarm clanging away in the shop. I pushed him into the back seat, and Damon pulled away, too fast.
'Damon,' I said.
'I hate those fucking alarms,' he said. But he slowed down, hung a left as the lights were changing, and tooled along gently towards the parking garage two blocks away where he had left the other car.

Hart was mumbling away next to me, his head in his hands.
'Ah, Jesus, I'm so sorry about that, I let you down completely in there, what are you going to think of me now?'

'I think you ought to stick to fucking carpets,' I said. I was furious with the fuck.

He stared at me miserably for a moment.

'I'm very sorry but I think I'm going to be sick,' he said.

I thought, please God, not in the Fenwick's bag, not on all the pretty jewels. He looked round wildly for a moment then pulled his brown felt hat off and buried his face in it.

Talk about class.

Back in the old days coming away from a rob we would all be so high, maybe a bit on stuff but mostly on the thing itself, screaming with laughter and often as not with Damon driving and Mick in the front next to him, Bruno and I in the back would start to fuck just because we were so high on it all and all four of us giggling and Damon's face laughing in the mirror and Mick craning round his face upside down so desperate he'd miss the least little last little detail, and all of us laughing all of us mad fucks deep friends mad fucks die for each other.

And here I was having to play the sensible one, sitting in my Donna Karan dress trying not to listen to my partner in crime being sick in his hat.

And here I am now, on this green hill watching the wind lift the grass and wishing I had acted otherwise.

Damon bounced the car up the ramp in the parking garage and there was a nice little blue Vauxhall Nova waiting for us. Hart lifted his face out of his hat. Tears were running down his cheeks and strings of stuff dangling from his nose and mouth, he looked like a little kid. 'Jesus I'm so sorry about that,' he said, 'I'm covered with confusion, I let you down completely. That's never happened to me before, never. I don't know what to say.'

'Well shut the fuck up then,' I said. I felt a bit mean, but then I thought he was lucky it was just me and Damon, if he'd bottled out on Bruno Bruno would probably have shot the fuck.

Damon pulled in next to the Nova and we got out. There was no one on our level. We got into the Nova. I sat in the front this time. I put my hat and glasses in the bag and took out a red sweat top and red woollen cap and pulled them on. Hart was snuffling away to himself in the back. I turned round. He was still holding his brown Christies hat upside down on his knees as if it was the Holy Grail instead of a hatful of puke.

'You were brilliant in there,' he said.

'Oh, wipe your nose,' I said.

'I haven't a hanky,' he said.

I thought Alan should be here, he always has paper tissues in his pocket for mopping up his little kids. He'd probably enjoy cleaning up this great big miserable fuck. It's OK, he'd tell him, it's OK. Everything is going to be OK.

We went through the exit and Damon paid the guy. The guy never looked at us. 'Eleven pounds forty,' said Damon as we headed west. 'Daylight robbery.'

We dropped John Hart at Queensway.

'See you,' he said, as he got out of the car.

'In your hole you will, my friend,' said Damon as we pulled away.

Damon dropped me on the corner of Portland Road. He had a meet planned at three with the guy who was going to buy the jewellery, which was all in Damon's little shoulder bag now. Three o'clock. It seemed like fucking years away. Damon wanted us to go for a drink but I was so disillusioned with the whole escapade I thought I'd just as soon go back to work.

The lampposts in Portland Road have these green litter bins on them. The first one I came to was packed full but the second one was empty. No one was looking. I jammed the Fenwick's bag into it. Then I remembered Hart had left his gun in it. I reached into the bag and got it out. I still don't know why I did that: I'm not normally a waste not want not sort of person.

I looked at my watch as I let myself into the office. The whole thing had only taken thirty-seven minutes.

A

Without telling Beatrice, I applied for a job up North. There were a hundred and seventy applicants but I had a strong feeling it was mine for the taking.

Bythwaite, the place was called. North Yorkshire. Swaledale, ten miles up from Reeth. I knew the place, sort of. We'd been for holidays in the Dales when I was little, renting this tumble-down stone cottage up the track from Low Row. I remembered steep scraggy hills and my legs getting tired, falling down a hole in Aysgarth and coming up with my boots full of little fishes. Getting washed on the kitchen table, standing naked on the kitchen table with my feet in the washing-up bowl, under the oil lamp, with a fire of logs spattering then blazing, nice sleepy glowing feeling, stepping out of the bowl on to thick wadded newspaper, with the big soft towel wrapped round me. I must have been about three then . . . that cottage had no bathroom, no hot water. My parents were still young and poor then, well not rich anyway, and there was this other couple too at that time staying with us with their kids, and, yes, there was, I realised later, something going on with the two couples. I could never seem to get my mother to myself, and if I woke up in the night and came down the creaky wooden staircase into the faintly smoky oil-lit glow of the living room it would always be Mummy and Alex cosily murmuring on the leaky old horsehair sofa, because Daddy and Elaine were down at the pub, or it would be Daddy and Elaine babysitting us because it was Mummy and Alex's turn at the pub. And then the year after that it was different: three of them would go out and one would stay home, or the two Daddies would go out and the two

Mummies stay home. And the year after that we didn't go with the Stevensons, or indeed to Yorkshire at all.

But I'd kept a sort of feel of the place in my mind: I think it was there that I might have first started playing my Captain Scarlet game, high up on the heathery moor above the pale green hills where the sheep clustered, high up where the grouse sat on walls and called to me 'Go back! Go back!' Nick must have been there but I don't remember him there at all. I do remember standing by Daddy on the dry stone wall in the early morning, both of us with our cocks out pissing in proud silver arches, feeling bold, careless, somehow outside the law, our hot juice hissing into the cold dry tussocky grass.

I took a coach to Darlington and then two more buses. It took most of the day. Stayed at the Bythwaite pub, sat in the bar where my father must have sat with Elaine Stevenson and my mother with Uncle Alex. There were two young couples in the bar, both very quiet. They had that air of social awkwardness and wariness covering a shared private sensuality, a sort of pale heat coming off them that I liked and identified with. One of the young men saw me looking and looked hard back at me. I sort of nodded at him, then got my book out of my pocket to show I meant no harm. If I get this job, I thought, we'll come in here for a drink, me and Beatrice, we'll be regulars, and if anyone looks at her I'll look at him like that. We won't want any friends because we will be everything to each other.

The school was timewarp: stonebuilt, squat, on the green. Bythwaite Combined, it was called. The kids looked sweet and thoughtful and slow moving compared to the twitchy London kids I was used to. I had a good feeling about it: I wasn't nervous at all. I felt about it something of what I felt the first time I saw Beatrice: this is it. This is for me.

There were three others on the shortlist: all women. I was used to that. They had got a little conversation started before I joined them in the waiting room; I let them talk and tried to look pleasant. They were all from the local area and knew each other. They kept sneaking looks at me. I was used to that too.

Each of us had to teach a sample ten-minute lesson to a class of seven-year-olds. The children sat round-eyed at their tables, seeming awed by their importance in the process of selection. At the back of the room, their broad beams overhanging the infants' chairs, six governors. I felt full of power, like a great hypnotist. I was tempted to launch into one of my exploratory-quest stories with them, but I did instead the thing I had prepared, a little mathematical event about symmetry and patterns and predictability, letting them discover the mysterious elegance of that silken web that holds us all together and stops us falling off the world. Watched their faces change as they guessed right, then suddenly saw why. One of the governors, a big heavy-faced man in a dark suit with loud troubled breathing, suddenly said 'Oh yes!' and then blushed scarlet when everyone turned to look at him. I think I might have been the teacher he always wished he'd had. Lovely, those rare times when it goes as well as that. Timing it, dropping the right words in, seeing the heads come up, the eyes widen, holding them back then letting them fly: excellent, excellent. Sometimes you think: this might be enough, on its own.

I don't remember a lot about the interview itself: I sensed that all I had to do was not fuck up; my only problem was I seemed that day too good to be true. None of them could pluck up the nerve to ask me if I was gay or a child molester, so I volunteered that I was eager to come to the area not only because of the happy childhood memories etcetera, but because my fiancée and I felt we had done our time in the inner city and now we wanted to have babies in a good safe place. You could see their bodies change in a comfortable relieved sort of thigh-shifting way.

I was telling the truth; why should I have felt such a fraud? Then I remembered that I was telling the truth only for myself. I hadn't asked Beatrice if she wanted to leave London.

I went back to the waiting room and sat with the three women who were quiet now and subdued, not looking at me any more. It was only five minutes before the heavy door swung open and they asked me to come in again.

Later, I stood next to Heavy Face and we pissed together, not on to cold tussocky grass but the solid porcelain of a serious nineteenth-century urinal.

'You were streets ahead of those women, Alan,' he told me. 'Streets ahead. Before you came we were saying your reference was so good you must be a wrong 'un, but no, you showed us otherwise. I've got a cottage you could rent, I'll let you have it cheap, I'm sick of these short holiday lets, I like things settled.' He stood back, shook the drops off his cock in a deliberate thorough way. 'Fancy a drink?'

We went and had a few pints in the pub. He told me how his wife had died two years ago, and how it had opened up strange and unexpected avenues for him, broadened his horizons in ways he would never have foreseen. He asked me if I had ever felt inclined to go round the wicket myself, and after a moment's puzzlement I said I hadn't. He said the offer of the cottage still stood.

Going back next day on the coach I was desperate to see her, desperate to tell her and for her to agree. Now I had made the move, applied for the job and got it, I couldn't bear to stay in London any more. I wanted to marry her. I wanted her to have my babies. I wanted us to do it in this slow strong clean place where she had no history.

A1, M1. I thought I could see and feel the air sludging up, the oily grime settle like an extra skin. Riding the sweaty tube in my interview suit, swimming up the escalator and out into the soupy air, wading across Shepherds Bush Green, I began to feel the hollow papery feeling. Suppose she turned from the window and stared at me blankly. Suppose she said Alan, you must be fucking crazy imagining I'd live in some godforsaken place like that, you don't know the first fucking thing about me do you? I hadn't even worked out what she would do till she had the baby, what jobs there might be there, no film production companies anyway that was for sure, and she was proud of her job; didn't exactly love it, but she loved something about herself in it: ASSISTANT ASSISTANT tell those fuckers where they get off! All that. Who was I to drag her off?

Captain Scarlet, that's who.

I ran up the stairs and opened the door and she was standing there facing the door looking tense as if she had been expecting it to be someone else, but when she saw it was me she ran to me and put her arms around my neck. I held her tight. She was pressing against me so hard it was as if she was trying to permeate me, get inside my skin. She pushed me against the door, her legs entwined around me. *Inside! Inside!*

'Listen,' I said.
　'I missed you,' she said. 'Don't leave me again.'
　'I don't want to leave you,' I said. 'I want to marry you.'
　'Yes, good,' she said. 'Let's get married. That's good.'
　'I've got a job,' I said. 'In Yorkshire.'
　'That's good,' she said. 'Let's go there.'
　'Really?'
　'Yes, yes, soon.'
　'You don't mind leaving your job?'
　'I hate it. Bunch of fucking wankers. Let's go tonight.'
　'We can have a baby,' I said. 'Shall we do that?'
　'Yes. Yes. Immediately.'
　'Well I understand it takes nine months or so.'
　'OK, whatever. Soon as possible. We could have a fucking brilliant baby, you and me.'

She was squirming against me, laughing. I started to laugh as well.
　'Come on,' she said. 'Fuck me.'
　'Look,' I said. 'I'm serious. I mean it.'
　'Fuck me. Give me a baby.'
　'Look,' I said. 'It's not a game.'
　'Oh, it is,' she said. 'It's all a game, really.'

I didn't know what she meant. I didn't know quite how she was feeling. I couldn't seem to tune in to her mood. She had a strange look in her eyes as if she was somewhere else as well as where we were.

'What is it?' I said.

'Oh, Alan,' she said. 'You're so fucking straight it sometimes makes me want to cry.'

She was leaning against me hard. She wasn't squirming any more, but she was still holding me very tight.

'It's *not* a game,' I said. I sounded about seven years old. 'I really have got a job. I really do want us to get married. And have a baby.'

'I know,' she said. 'It's OK. Let's do it.'

B

So we did it.

I couldn't wait.

Partly my dear one and wanting to get on with it, but partly stupid stuff, stupid Fucknose stuff. I was a bad girl when Alan went away.

Well I was feeling insecure. I thought it was strange him having secrets from me, not telling me where he was going or why. I never thought he might be shagging anyone. He would never make me worry in that way. What I thought, I thought he might be going to see his family and he was ashamed to show me to them, but it wasn't that.

That came later.

I got in from work and had a beer and sat around thinking what I should do and wondering where he was and what he was doing and what he was thinking about. And then I started to wonder what it was like to be him when he was not with me, and whether he carried me round with him in his head and whether his cock remembered me (cock memory, like muscle memory for ice skating or horse riding, like my cunt memory for his sweet particular moves) or whether he was just like he was before he knew me, that straight tense striver on his racing bike. And I thought: the latter, probably.

My dear one is naive and he is innocent and I had to teach him how to fuck me properly, and there are whole heaving oceans of this life that he knows shit about, but there is this one big thing: he knows who he is and he is all right on his own.

And I don't, really, and I'm not.

I put pasta on to boil, with salt and a bit of olive oil in the water. I chopped up some mushrooms and fried them in butter with garlic and tarragon and after a bit I tipped in a carton of *fromage frais* I found lurking in the fridge. Grated cheese. Black pepper. Little slag from the gutter, cooks like Elizabeth fucking David. *Read my name.* Had another beer with that. I was feeling dead mature. B. Monkey in control.

I thought what I would do, I'd have this really civilised evening on my own. Put on some music and read a Shakespeare play. I only know one myself and that is *Macbeth*. Good things of day begin to droop and drowse. Light thickens. Brilliant. Alan is keen on one called *Troilus and Cressida*, well, he's mentioned it a couple of times. I thought it would be cool if I read up on it, then when he came back, I could say: oh by the way, I was re-reading *Troilus and Cressida* the other night, and I was really struck by . . . well, some fucking thing or another. And he would look at me and his eyes would widen in delight and admiration of his brilliant girlfriend.

What a load of horseshit; I couldn't get past the first page. There seemed to be too much you had to know already, for a start, and too much bollocking about with tarrying and leavening and baking and cooling and the princes orgulous . . . I needed help, I needed therapy, I needed someone to lead me to the good bits. What I really needed was to go to college, go to fucking university. Well, why not? I got two A levels. Do a couple of sub post-offices, pay my own fucking fees.

That made me remember John Hart's gun. It was in the cupboard stuffed into one of my boots. I got it out and started messing about with it. Guns are . . . strangely heavy . . . they're rather fine things in a way, so carefully made, the bits fitting so neatly together. All that care and patience that goes into making them, and then people use them for ripping great holes through other people's skin and muscle and the poor red pulsing parts inside, that were not made to be invaded. It was making me feel strange, the gun. I looked at my watch. It was only half past seven. I phoned Paul. He was in. I told him I was coming round, I had a present for him.

I phoned a minicab. Just go there and back, I told myself. Maybe have just the one. Get back and have an early night. No sweat. Magic.

The big mansion blocks on Prince of Wales Drive loomed up like ocean liners, speckled with lights at the windows. I paid the driver and went in. It felt like coming home.

We had some beers. I told him Alan was away and I was only staying half an hour. Paul said that was fine, it was lovely to see me. I asked him how he was and he said that he was missing me. I told him about trying to read *Troilus and Cressida* and how fucking useless it had made me feel and he told me I was useful to him because I was a sweet girl and a reason to be cheerful. That made me feel nice.

He sat down at his piano and he played one of his songs on the parts of the piano that were still in tune. He sang in his scratchy smoked-out voice:

> The way you hold your knife
> The way we danced till three
> The way you changed my life . . .

I said I had to go. He said: I'll tell you what, why don't you take your clothes off, we'll do a line of coke and I'll give you a stroke. I said no, I really have to go now.

We did a few lines of coke and then I took my clothes off. I showed him the gun, showed him how it worked. I told him I thought he should have it: even if he never used it it would give him a kind of confidence. He turned it over and over in his hands. He said: when I was young, I had absolutely no idea my life was going to be like this.

We had another beer and did a little more cocaine and he asked me if I would like to stay the night, as Alan was in Yorkshire. I said no, really, I think it would be best to go back, I would call another minicab.

We took the gun to bed with us and played about with it a bit. I said to myself: this is all right really, I could probably explain it all to Alan and he would understand, that Paul is really like a sort of daddy, a sort of fucked up daddy who can't quite make it on his own and needs a girl to help. And I am a girl with the same sort of problem.

I suppose we went to sleep then, because the next thing I knew was waking up and knowing there was someone in the flat.

I sat up in bed just as they came into the room. Two men in suits, on the big side. They didn't say anything. They just stood there staring. I suppose they had not expected me to be there.

Paul sat up on one elbow.
    'You again,' he said. 'Christ, what a bore.'
    Paul was cool and arrogant in a way that did him no fucking good at all. You could see them quivering to hurt him.
    'Are these the ones that came before?' I said.
    'I'm afraid so,' he said. 'I'm sorry, darling. They're really awful men. I can't think of a single thing to say in their favour.'

You could see them both trying to think of something devastatingly witty and frightening to say. One of them was older than the other, a bit of a has-been, short and squat and tired looking. The younger one was the main man, tall and pale with nasty sandy-coloured hair and freckles, a thin prim mouth, faintly reminiscent of Steve Davis.

'Shut up, cunt. You're dead,' said this one to Paul. Not too brilliant, considering he'd had time to think. I was feeling brilliantly alert myself. I was looking forward to the next few moments.
    'Who are you then?' Steve Davis asked me.
    'I'm his fucking bodyguard, son,' I said. I got the gun out from under the pillow, and aimed it at Steve, holding it steady in both hands the way they do it in the movies. I was getting this terrible urge to laugh, and fighting it down. They were staring at me as if they couldn't believe it. I suppose it must have been

like a bad dream for them. They didn't know whether to stare at my tits or the gun.

'Take it off her, Joe,' said Steve Davis. 'It's a fucking toy.'
 Joe started to move, very tentatively. Hardly a step.
 'It's real,' I said. Joe stopped and looked at Steve.
 'Take it off the bitch,' said Steve. 'She can't shoot both of us.'
 'Don't you believe it,' I said. And then, to my great surprise, I aimed at his belly and pulled the trigger. The gun jumped in my hand, I heard a bang, but faint, like an echo, and he fell down, holding his leg. I had aimed for his belly and hit him in the leg. Harder than it looks, believe me, shooting people. I aimed at Joe. Middle of his chest this time. Bigger target. My hands were trembling, but only a bit.

'Benny,' said Paul. 'Chaps. Time to reflect.'

'She fucking shot me,' said Steve Davis. 'Look. Look at all this blood.'
 'It's your own fault,' said Paul. 'You shouldn't have come in here and frightened us.'
 'Let's kill them,' I said. 'Let's get this over with. I want to get some sleep.'
 I sounded really good, hard and strong and cruel, but I was feeling very strange, as if I was dreaming. I thought I might be going to do a John Hart and faint or puke but no one had a hat.
 'Please,' said the man called Joe. 'This has got all out of hand.'

Someone was knocking on the flat door.
 'Paul? Are you all right?'
 'Just the guy upstairs,' said Paul. He called to the man: 'I'm fine! Sorry about that! Frightful noise but no damage, sorry to disturb you!'
 'Are you sure you're OK?'
 'Absolutely, thanks, fine!'
 We waited for a while and heard the flat door close upstairs.

The young one got up slowly.
 'Don't come any nearer,' I said. I was still holding the gun in both hands. My wrists were getting tired.
 'I think you should go now,' said Paul. 'Can you walk?'
 'Yes,' said Steve Davis. 'Enough.'

'Tell your chap to call you off. This is ridiculous, all this. He'll get his money, he knows that, he just has to learn to be patient like the rest of us. Tell him that, would you?'

'Yeah, all right.'

'Tell him I want him to reimburse me for the piano.'

'Yeah, all right.'

'OK. Off you go, then.'

He turned round at the door, the tall one, the Steve Davis one. He pointed at me.

'You are fucking dead,' he said.

I couldn't understand why everything was escalating so fast. What is that word that Alan likes so much?

Exponential.

Yes.

A

I wanted them to see her, just once. I didn't need them to like her and I certainly didn't need her to like them. I just wanted them to see her. I wanted them to see what we had.

And I thought it might be interesting for her to get a look at them.

As it happened, we got a bit more than we expected. Nick was there as well, with his new girlfriend. That was OK. In fact I loved it, the way Nick couldn't take his eyes off her and seemed consumed with curiosity about her, whereas she didn't seem to be the slightest bit interested in him, or the woman with him. Excellent, excellent. *And* I beat him at chess too. Humiliated him, in fact. Two straight victories, his king trapped and screaming in my powerful and subtle net. His girlfriend, Carla, stayed and watched right through, though I don't think she understood much about chess. I think she might have understood the game we were playing, though.

Beatrice went for a walk with my father while Nick and I were playing chess. She didn't say what they talked about, if anything. They seemed to get on quite well with each other, which I must admit surprised and rather disappointed me. It wasn't that she was impressed by his eminence or anything. It wouldn't matter a fuck to her whether a person was interviewed on *Newsnight* or not. No, she seemed to sort of *like* him, in a way. I suppose I was rather hoping she would see him as an utterly irredeemably self-deluding poseur, and marvel how such a prince of men as her beloved could have sprung from such morally shoddy loins.

167

My mother was, well, difficult. But when was she anything else?

We stayed the night, just the one night. I wanted to do that. We stayed in my old room, the room I had had as a boy. They had done it up a bit as a guest room, new curtains and so on, but they had kept my old bed. The room still emitted a powerful essence of what it had been. It still sang to me of loneliness and hopeless dreams, acne and solitary sex. It was like a sacramental gift to fuck with my dear one in my old bed, my boy's bed. I told her how I had stained the sheets with my first wet dream, woken in a panic, and been found by my mother in the middle of the night trying to sponge out the acrid effluent that had exploded out of my insurrectionary member. My mother is of course one of that school of children's writers who tenderly celebrate the subtle mysteries of the menarche, the blossoming of the pubic bush, the Feast of the Descending of the Testicles, but she finds fiction more comfortable to handle than reality, I think, and her warm vibrant efforts to be intuitive and practical, concerned but not intrusive, practical yet offhandedly tender, made me want to howl like a banshee. I would have preferred her to call me a dirty little sod and leave it at that. She – well, let's say she didn't make it easy for me on that significant and memorable night. Not so surprising, now, then, that I would have liked to leave the bedclothes positively festooned with jissom, the mattress soaked right through with my darling's cunt juice. I wished that night that I was a noisier comer: I would have liked to roar in orgasm like a bull elephant, with my darling's little high cries ringing out above in heartstoppingly beautiful counterpoint. I would have liked everyone I've ever known to file through the room and contribute their vociferous applause. But as it was, it was wonderful. A catharsis, a celebration, and a milestone.

Something unfortunate and sort of *stupid*, really, happened on the Sunday morning. My father slipped and fell in his study, banged his nose on the edge of his desk. We thought he might have broken it. My mother had to drive him to Casualty, so we had rather a hurried parting. Just as well, perhaps, really. Slipping and falling and hurting yourself. It's what toddlers and old people do. I had a little pang, watching them go off in the car, a sort of queasy feeling around the scrotal zone. He was leaning on her, a bit, with his jacket elegantly draped around his shoulders, dark glasses, white silk hanky pressed against his face. He was leaning on her, and she too looked as if she could have done with someone to lean on, as if all her carry-on had been a scared child's testing-out of love. I suddenly saw my parents as quite small and vulnerable. My father's fifty-eight now. That's not old. It's the prime of life, that's what he says. See his photo in the Education *Guardian*, see him mash up the hostile interviewer on the regional TV news: deep voice, noble profile, the fierce beard jutting beneath the confident smile. Yes, I know, all hollow, all a pose, grandiloquent self-regarding horseshit, yes yes yes, thinking all that is how I have always protected myself from him. But to see him on Sunday morning, kind of drawn into himself, I think it was to see the beginning of his dying. He looked frail, unsure, out of it, somehow.

Both of them. The backs of their heads in the car. Small, and vulnerable, getting smaller all the time as the car went away down the road.

B

Get me out of here.

I don't know if it's them or me but it is getting worse.

I can't believe it, what they were like, what happened, what I did. No sense to it. The things that I do, what are they trying to tell me?

He came to meet my mum and he was very sweet. She thought he was lovely. She got a bit pissed. We told her about going to Yorkshire, and she cried.

Nothing to be done. Being sad is like a job for her. I'm not her ectoplasm any more.

And then we went to meet his famous fucking parents at last and it was a very strange visit indeed, for Beatrice Monkey.

What I did, I freaked out a bit, and no one knows about it except Alan's father.

First of all I got very daunted by the house and all the doings, all the posh snobs, all the books and fucking wine and that, don't ask me why, I've been around, with Paul especially, I've had the waiters scurrying, I've shot the shit in flasher gaffs than Freddie Furnace's, places with bodyguards and stableblocks, so what was the matter with me? I'd never come across this particular sort of Oxfordy bullshit before, but it's basically just like the other sorts of bullshit, namely bullshit. If they're talking over your head, yawn in their fucking faces, that's my motto, they need you more than you need them is what I usually find.

And they were quite nice to me, or seemed to be, well his father was, or seemed to be. I don't know what it was, I just got all shy and clammed up. His brother was there, the writer, bit of a flash git, leather jacket, black curly hair, make a lovely waiter in an Italian restaurant, but all fucked up inside. All fucked up and nowhere to go. Sort of a desperate striver, frantically not at rest. Forget it. He wanted to know whether by any chance I'd read anything of his. I managed to mutter no. Oh, he said, pity. He did a little sidelong glance at Alan, implying of course that reading his stuff would give me deep and otherwise inaccessible insights into his strange young brother. What a prick. I only needed five minutes to know I wouldn't be interested in reading anything that fuck-up had to say. So why was I too shy to speak to him or even properly to look at him?

Fucknose.

He had a tall girl with him, Carla, very beautiful, one of those long soft bodies, she looked . . . yeah, *cosseted*. I've seen plenty of girls like her, mostly in the big houses with the high walls and the closed shutters and the guard dogs in the Paris suburbs, but there was someone else she reminded me of, someone specific, that I couldn't quite place . . . She seemed OK in a way though, Carla, gave me these little friendly glances like saying here we are, we're the chicks, we're the girlies of this situation, let's not give each other a hard time, we're paid-up members of the girly union from *way* back, but I was so choked up for some reason I couldn't give her back the sort of eye she wanted.

The mother talked the whole time, the whole fucking time, at me, really, mostly, about this book she was writing about deprived kids in the inner city and how she'd discovered this paradoxical phenomenon that in this racist society of ours the delinquents and the dispossessed were colour-blind, the inner city was full of disaffected but totally racially integrated gangs in which *girls* would you believe it were playing an increasingly important role. Not just for shagging, I think she meant. She was telling me about stuff I knew but I still couldn't, still couldn't . . . ah, shit. Then she asked me what it was I did for a living now, though I knew Alan had told her, I thought she's like a missionary talking to a savage, and it's my own fucking fault: I muttered 'secretary' with my chin in my chest. I didn't even have the spirit to say assistant. She said oh.

Then Alan's father started twinkling at me. 'Alan tells me you used to be something of a graffiti artist. I'm very interested. Public buildings? Lavatories?'

'Walls and trains mostly,' I managed to mutter.

'Walls and trains! The big league!'

He did know something then. I started to find my tongue.

'Nothing too fancy, really. Spray-can stuff. You've seen the sort of stuff. Just um just marking out the territory really. Signatures.'

'Like academic publishing,' he said. 'Inner-city walls and trains, the refereed journals of the underclass.'

He was a prat, but sort of interesting with it. I was starting to relax. A little soft Fucknosey voice began to whisper in my ear: what's the stupidest possible thing you could do in this house this weekend?

Alan's mother, Frances, was turning her head impatiently this way and that, she'd had the conversation snatched away from her and she wanted to bite it back. But she couldn't see the way to do it.

'I've probably read your name without realising it,' said Alan's father.

'B. Monkey,' I said. 'That was my street name.'

'A street name!' That was the brother. 'How gorgeous! I bet you never had a street name, Carla!'

I didn't even look at him.

'Fancy a game of chess after lunch, Nick?' said Alan.

'Yes,' the brother said. 'All right. To the death?'

'To the death,' said Alan.

God, I thought, why has he dragged me along, this is all nothing to do with me.

'So, Beatrice, what else did you do besides write graffiti on walls and trains – or is that a full-time occupation? – forgive my ignorance . . .?'

'God, Mother . . .' muttered Alan.

'I'm sorry, darling?'

'Nothing. Nothing.'

'I was a criminal, I suppose,' I said.

She stared at me.

'A *criminal*? In what sense?'

'Well in the sense I used to do robberies,' I said, 'and utter threats, and drive away vehicles without the consent of their owners, you know, crimes, crimes against property, crimes against the person.'

She didn't know how to deal with it. She didn't know whether to believe me or not.

'I've given it up now,' I said. 'I'm a secretary now. Well, assistant actually. That's like a secretary, only flasher.'

Alan started to giggle. I jabbed him in the ribs with my elbow but it only made him giggle more.

'And you and Alan are thinking of . . . *getting married*?'

'We are married,' said Alan. 'Meet the wife, Mum.'

He was giggling so much now he was purple in the face.

'I'm sorry,' he said. 'I'm sorry. It's just . . . I'm sorry.'

See me, after lunch, not helping carry out the dishes to the kitchen. But his mother did manage to draw me aside for a private word. 'Beatrice, dear,' she said. 'I do hope you're not expecting a long heart-to-heart mother-daughter sort of *chat* thing?' I said no, I didn't have any expectations really. 'Thank you,' she said. 'That kind of intimacy just isn't my style somehow. And anyway I have to work this afternoon. Work – the sort of work I do – has to come first. You sacrifice every-thing. Nick understands. I hope you do too.'

'Um yeah' was all I could muster up in response to that one, and with that, she fucked off upstairs to her study, the great thoughts already rampant in her fevered brain no doubt.

The rest of us went in the living room. It was big and shabby and full of books and, fuck me, yes, a *piano*, a piano with photos in frames. I found this one of the family when Alan was about three. He had this little round face and he looked happy and looked-after. And his mum and dad looked young, and nice, and full of hope somehow. Nick was about eleven, in his little flared jeans, staring out to the side of the frame, looking as if he had worries of his own.

I sat down on one of the exhausted-looking beigey old sofas. There was a dog asleep on the other one, one of those shiny chestnut-coloured setter things, sort of a flash country dog. Nick started getting out the chess set in a theatrically grim and portentous way, as if he and Alan were in a suicide pact or something. Alan sat down opposite him. Carla arranged herself in a very chickly and decorative manner on the arm of Nick's chair. I thought fuck that for a lark. I picked up the *Independent* and read about how some new restaurant in Brook Green had tragically disappointed the expectations of the cognoscenti, and what a shrewd move it would be to buy a two-year-old Renault 25 with f.s.h., whatever that might be. A huge wave of boredom so desperate it was like panic washed over me, and without really meaning to, I let out a great groaning sigh, and the dog woke up and blinked at me.

'Fancy a walk, Beatrice?' said Alan's father.
    The dog started leaping around barking.
    'Yeah, all right,' I said.
    'I noticed you'd brought your walking boots,' he said.
    'Those are my kicking boots,' I said. He smiled.
    'Anyone else?'
    It seemed to me he didn't sound too eager; and Carla smiled and shook her head. Alan and Nick didn't even lift theirs.
    'OK,' he said. 'Let's go.'

It wasn't much of a walk. We got in his car, he had a big old Citroën, and he drove to the edge of these woods and pulled off the road on to the soft grassy verge. The dog, Kate, went charging off into the bracken.

I'd only been in a wood once or twice before. It's strange. The way it gets darker when you go in, you feel you ought to talk a bit more softly, like in church or something, and it is a bit like a church, that sort of browny goldy light.

Fucknose was starting to whisper in my ear again, and just to say anything, I asked him: 'What's it like then, being a professor?'

'It's all right,' he said. 'It's a game, really. I feel a bit of a fraud sometimes.'

'I was thinking maybe I should go to university,' I said. 'I've got two A levels.'

'No problem then,' he said.

'They're only Es,' I said.

'No problem,' he said. 'Not if you'd like to go to Oxford.'

Fuck me, I thought, I've fallen on my feet here. He kept looking at me, sort of searching my face, we were walking along, but he never stopped looking at me, his head turned right round, I thought he'll walk into a tree in a minute. (He wants your cunt, said Fucknose.)

'You're really remarkable, Beatrice. But you know that, don't you?' he said. (See? said Fucknose.) 'I think it's absolutely amazing how Alan managed to find you.'

'You don't think *he's* remarkable?' I said.

He stopped, so really I had to stop too. Well, I did stop.

'Yes,' he said. 'I do think he's remarkable. And I love him very much.'

Yes, I thought, I think you do. And so do I. So what's all this?

'Look,' he said. 'I have to do this.' He reached out, and took hold of my left breast, quite gently, outside my shirt.

I just stood still. I let him do it. I wasn't scared. I didn't feel under any pressure. I just let him do it. Don't ask me why. I think mostly I was just very interested what would happen next.

He moved his hand slowly, taking my nipple between his thumb and his forefinger. I thought, you've done that before. He had this sort of rapt expression, like a great scientist on the brink of a discovery. I found I was excited. Even starting to get a little damp down there.

'This is terrible,' he said. 'Ah . . . what happens next?'

'Don't know,' I said.

He moved in closer.

'No kissing,' I said.

'What, then?' he said.

'Don't know,' I said.

He took my hand, and pressed it against the front of his brown cords. I looked around. There was no one about. I could see flashes of chestnut brown in a clearing a little way off: Kate chasing birds.

'I wouldn't mind a look at it,' I said.

He gave a little gasp.

'Are you sure you're up to this?' I said.

'Yes! Yes! Christ.'

I unzipped his trousers and took him in my hand. Quite big, like Alan. Smooth and silky. Strange, the way they don't age the way that faces do. So innocent-looking. I thought, how extraordinary: Alan came out of there.

I looked up at his face. Alan's father. Freddie. He had his rapt scientist expression on again.

'Thanks,' I said.

'Christ,' he said, 'what d'you mean? Thank *you*.'

'You're welcome.'

'Look, he said. 'We can't just leave it like that.'

'Yes, we can,' I said.

Two people with a black dog suddenly came out of the clearing, and down the path towards us. 'Jesus Christ!' said Freddie, whirling round. He seemed to be having trouble cramming himself back in, and I started laughing. Kate came romping back, sniffed my hand thoroughly, stared in my face, and sneezed. 'Come on,' I said. 'Let's go. I want a cup of tea.'

Ah, Fucknose, Fucknose, what you do to me. Fortunately Freddie and Frances, as I was now instructed to call them, were out to dinner that night. Nick, in a bad mood after the chess duel, drove Carla back to Muswell Hill. So my young husband and I went down the local pub and held hands. When we got back, his parents were still out. I wanted to avoid them. Freddie had been smiling at me in this awful sort of knowing and yet pleading way ever since we got back, I had been stupid stupid *stupid* when when *when* will I get *sensible*? So I said let's go to bed now and not wait up for them. I thought Alan might think that was a bit rude, but he didn't seem to.

I woke up quite early. I was starving. We'd only had crisps down the pub. Alan was still asleep, so I went downstairs to see what I could find in the fridge.

Freddie was in the kitchen sitting at the table. He jumped up when I came in and said: 'Thank Christ. I've been willing you to come down. I've been here since a quarter to five.'

'Don't start,' I said. 'I'm just looking for something to eat.'

He grabbed hold of me.

'Listen,' he said. 'I've never felt like this before. I'm bloody desperate for you.'

'Don't be stupid,' I said. 'Get off me.'

He let go and I started cutting and buttering a slice of bread.

'I've been awake all night,' he said. 'What are we going to do about this?'

'Nothing,' I said.

'Jesus!' he said. 'But what about yesterday afternoon? Did that mean nothing to you?'

'For fuck's sake, Freddie,' I said. 'I only took a look at it. Let's just forget about it, OK?'

He went very quiet for a moment and then he said: 'I think perhaps we have to discuss the whole thing with Alan: how would that be?'

I thought, you fuck. I picked up the heavy glass lid of the butterdish and smacked him in the nose with it.

'You say a word to Alan, I'll put you in fucking hospital,' I said. He believed me all right.

The blood was coming out of his nose now. He sat down.

'Christ,' he said. 'It hurts.'

'I'm sorry,' I said. 'I didn't really mean to hurt you.'

'No,' he said. 'My fault, I asked for it. It bloody well hurts though.'

I looked at him, sitting there. I did feel sorry. I think I'm getting soft in my old age. Hope for me yet.

Professor Freddie Furnace.

Get me out of here.

A

Waking early in the mornings, watching her sleep. On her front with her bottom in the air like a baby. On her back with one hand flung behind her head, her hand open, her fingers slightly curled, her arm completely relaxed as if she were anaesthetised . . . the little dark ringlet of hair in her armpit . . .

On her side facing me, on her side facing away from me . . .

The light is different here. The low clinging cloud, swollen with rain. The silences, the distances.

She curls her strong toes round my toes and holds them in her sleep. She loves me in her sleep.

B. Monkey.

Beatrice.

The silences, the distances.

What's worst is that when it really is OK, something down there is murmuring very quietly . . . I look in the mirror and I see my terrified grin.

I love her so much I think it might be bad for me.

This place though, it's almost perfect, almost the place I dreamed of taking her. A one-up, one-down cottage, semi-detached from a semi-ruined barn. With water and an ancient Aga to heat it. A single-track road climbs from the valley road at an improbably steep sharp angle and contorts itself in a double hairpin so violent you can't believe it the first few times. The road disappears entirely from view, dropping away sheerly to left and right, and as it disappears, you fling the wheel round sharply to the right in an act of blind faith, the back wheels skitter round, and up you go again. Then hard to the left, the same. Get it wrong one side, you scrape the wall. Get it wrong the other, you're tumbling down the bank. The road peters out only half a mile up the hill, where there used to be a little settlement, four or five cottages, all empty now, waiting to be restored for summer lets.

The road to our cottage is just a track worn by tractor wheels. We have a clapped-out Escort that gets up it in the dry, or just about. When it's wet we leave it where it stops and walk the rest of the way. When the baby comes we'll get a four-wheel-drive car. My father seems curiously eager to lend us, even give us, money. I feel reluctant to take it but Beatrice says why not, if he wants to. Don't worry about money, she says, money comes when you need it. Money is easy to get. This seems to me a strange thing to say, and not really in accordance with the facts, but I like it, somehow.

We're all alone up here. Down at the junction of the valley road, there's a garage, if that's not too grand a name for it. Basically it's just an old petrol pump and a big shed where a man called Jim Arkright can sometimes be found tinkering with an old tractor. There used to be a pottery as well with a little shop, but that failed. A phonebox, too remote from civilisation to be vandalised.

We read, we walk. Sometimes we go to the pub and sit together holding hands. We're not unfriendly, but I like to feel that we radiate a private sensuality, a sort of pale heat coming off us that discourages casual conversation. We are regulars. People accept us. We don't want any friends because we are everything to each other.

We have an outside toilet in its own little shed, an original two-holer, which I maintain in pristine condition, having read up on the subject in a book. It has a magnificent view over the valley, and sometimes, not always, we don't make a fetish of it, we sit together at this simplest of tasks.

This, too, is one of the times when I feel I love her almost more than I can bear. That simple sharing of herself she manages so easily, her brilliant open wholly trusting smile as she turns and reaches for the toilet paper.

The summer's almost gone now. Next week I start teaching in the little school. I'm looking forward to it.

So what am I anxious about? Why do I wake so early, from troubled dreams? Why do I brood about her silences, her absences, wonder where she is when she's asleep?

There is a strange greenish stain on the sofa by the window. I go to wipe it off with a J-cloth and I find that it is not in fact a stain, the whole sofa is rotting in a kind of gangrene, some kind of organic green slime with an agenda of its own. Viscous thick sticky puddles are forming on the carpet. The plants are melting too. I look down and find that my boots are beginning to disintegrate. The green stuff is all over my hands now and I cannot wipe it off.

What's the matter? Let me take your photo. Come on, please. What is it? What's the matter? Everything's OK. I promise. I promise. Everything will be OK.

B

Here, now, in this safe place he's made for me, I still feel as if I'm clinging by my fingertips. What's happened to B. Monkey? Where's the trip?

This place, it's deafeningly peaceful. You can hear a car coming from miles away.

We have no neighbours. Less than six people know we are here. Alan teaches in Bythwaite, fourteen miles away. I have no job. There's nothing to do. I piss about all day. When he comes home, we eat, we drink, we shag like rabbits. We are 'trying for a baby'. We are pretending that this is it, this is what it is, but both of us sense that it is temporary, that we are waiting for something to happen, and that we've chosen this place for it to happen in.

I can't see the river, but I can see the hawk hanging in the air above it. He's been here all day.

The gun hangs on the wall behind the kitchen door.

That's OK. That's fine. Everyone has guns up here. We went and took lessons, me and my dear one. I was the best in the class and Alan was the second best. We were proud of ourselves.

The killing that goes on up here. The people kill the animals and the animals kill each other. Last week I saw a strange thing: a rabbit stuck in a hole in a dry-stone wall. His front paws and his head were through and he was looking at me in an expectant sort of way, I thought. I thought he was stuck and he needed some sort of encouragement to wriggle free. I thought when I went over to him he'd panic and struggle out, but he didn't. So I gave him a tug and pulled him out.

Something had torn off his back legs from the other side of the wall.

Alan says: It's going to be OK, really, it's going to be OK.

Alan. He doesn't even know what it is, let alone whether it's going to be OK or not. My fault, really. I got him into this.

Though I never asked him to choose me.

The trick is: when you're in the scary place, try to be the scary monster. Even if it's just pretend.

I was walking with Alan's father through tussocky fields which led towards dunes and I could hear the sea but not see it. The clouds were blowing fast, fast across the sky and he said of course it's all up now, the Parati have taken over. I didn't know what the Parati were, it sounded like Italian to me and I don't know any Italian, and I asked are they political, and he laughed and said yes, in a way, he said not many people know about them, they're insects, actually, millions of them but with one single brain between them, and over the last ten years or so they've increased immeasurably, *exponentially*, starting in the sand of the beaches all round the island, and moving in slowly, an all-enveloping infestation, reproducing and producing new varieties at a frightening rate. Look, he said. He pointed down towards the dunes and I could see them. Soft rounded shapes I had mistaken for dunes were in fact made up of millions of these brown busy scrabbling creatures, eating everything they touched, and coming closer all the time. I could hear the rustle of their wings, their blind scurryings.

He turned and smiled at me. It was a funny smile. They're the most predatory creatures to evolve on earth, he said. They're even more predatory than we are. They're – how shall I put it – they're *the next thing*. After us, I mean. I find it rather comforting, in an odd sort of way, he said. To think that we're in the last few seconds of the history of the universe, but that there's something else coming after us. He smiled again. Not anything nice, of course, he said – but then, *we* weren't very nice, were we?

I started hitting him and yelling at him what a bastard and a shit he was, that just because he was all fucked up and ready to die, that didn't mean the rest of us were, and he laughed and grabbed my wrists and said you don't understand, you don't understand, what I'm saying is that this is what is going to happen whether you like it or not, and my arms and legs felt weak, I couldn't fight him, and he held both my wrists with one hand and unzipped his trousers with the other and took his prick out and forced it into my mouth, and as he pushed it in and out it felt cold and thin and hard and when I looked down I saw that it was made of glass like a thermometer and I heard it smash against my teeth and then I was crunching glass, and I could taste blood in my mouth and blood was running down my chin and then he looked and saw what had happened and started screaming.

I went down to the phonebox by the tractor garage today and gave Paul a buzz. I was sort of anxious about him. He answered the phone in a very guarded wary sort of way, I thought. I asked him how he was and he said fine. He didn't sound too good to me. I asked him if he was missing me and he said yes he was, he was yearning for me tragically. I said come on, Paul, life goes on. Don't give me a hard time. He said he knew that life went on but what he found so hard to bear was that he didn't know where I was, that he would never intrude on my life but that if he just knew that he could speak to me if he wanted he would be all right. I told him we didn't have a telephone, but I gave him the number of the callbox. I said if he just held on and let it ring, the guy in the garage would take a message and I'd get it eventually and I'd call him back. He said that he could envisage circumstances a bit more pressing than that. He asked if I would tell him how to get to the cottage, not that he imagined he would ever come, but it would temper the loss of me to be able to locate me geographically.

Ah, tell him, said Fucknose.

I asked him if he had paid those guys and settled all that business with Steve Davis and his mates and he said of course he had. I wasn't too convinced.

He asked me if we would give him shelter for the night if he was absolutely at his wits' end. What could I say? I said of course I would. I said Paul, if you have to come here, I have to take you in. He said you'd better tell me where it is, then.

Ah, well, I thought. Sooner or later it was going to happen. I walked up the hill with a heavy heart. The grouse were all sitting on the dry-stone wall above the cottage. Go back, they said. Go back.

Listen, I said to Alan when he came in from teaching his little kids. There are some things I think I have to tell you now.

Before I told Alan about Paul and his problem with the enforcers, I wanted to prepare the ground a bit: I wanted to make him understand how what had happened before kept coming back, outside of me and inside me as well, and how he had made me better but not perfect yet, and how I hoped he would be patient. There is a Beatrice I was and a Beatrice I am becoming, I told him. It isn't easy for me, I told him. He kept saying he didn't understand, so in the end I thought oh fuck it I'll just tell him stuff and hope for the best. Just remember, Alan, it was stuff before you, you should have come sooner, it would have been different, I would have been better then.

I tried to tell him about my first proper crime, which was all about making friends really. It was my first week in the unit, and I'd just got over being scared shitless of the hard boys and realised they liked me and thought I was cute and clever. We were all sitting on a wall in that little stub of Portland Road opposite the Britannia, me and Bruno and Damon, it was just about ten on a summer night, and the boys were just telling jokes, and I was listening and laughing, and none of us wanted to go home. And while we were sitting there, this dark blue Mercedes came down Clarendon looking for a parking place and hung a left and parked just about five yards away from where we were sitting on the wall. This old guy with white hair got out, and he had this really beautiful girl about twenty-five with him, and she wasn't his granddaughter, she was his girlfriend, you could tell. They were both pissed senseless. He took about ten goes to lock the car up, and she was propping herself up on the car waiting for him. She had one of those long soft bodies ... We were still laughing, and they thought we were laughing at them, because when they came past us, the guy stopped, and he looked at Bruno, and he said: 'What?' like that. As if we'd already been talking for a while. It was strange. But Bruno just said 'Is that your car?' and the old guy said 'Yes it is.' Then the girl said: 'Bet you wish you had one.' She had sort of a posh voice, like the old guy, but I knew straight away that she had once been like me, and still was, in a way. Bruno said: 'I wouldn't mind a drive in it,' and the old guy said: 'Not on, I'm afraid. You'll have one of your own one day.' He was quite friendly, really, the old guy, and so was Bruno, but the girl was dead aggressive.

We watched them go into one of the tall houses in Clarendon. Bruno said: 'Come on. I'm not fucking putting up with that.' We went over to the car. I didn't know what we were going to do. Bruno never even looked to see if anyone was coming, he just smashed the driver's side window and opened the doors. He tried to start it but he couldn't, so he took the radio and got out. 'Fucking Mercs, they're stubborn sods,' he said. 'Fuck it, I was just feeling like a little drive.' I was just staring open-mouthed. Start it or not, he'd impressed me all right. Then both the boys pissed on the seats through the open window. I'd never seen their pricks before, of course, and I thought they looked beautiful in the light from the street lamp, Damon's milk-chocolate-coloured one and Bruno's deathly pale one, and the twin streams of piss arching through the windows of the dark blue Mercedes. They tried to get me to piss in it as well, but I was too shy. I said I didn't know them well enough and anyway it's harder for a girl.

I think I'll always remember them, the old guy and the girl, I'm not sure why. I sometimes sort of wonder what happened to them, what they're doing now. Particularly the girl.

I thought it would be an easy one to start with, but it wasn't. I kept hesitating over whether to mention certain details that I thought might upset him or disgust him. Like the pissing in the car and the boys' cocks, I left all that bit out, but I think perhaps it might have been essential to the meaning of the story.

When I finished telling him he didn't say anything at all. I thought oh shit shit this has all been a mistake, and I remembered Paris and looking at my running-away money in my bag across the room, and how I found I couldn't run away from him because we were both trapped in it together.

Come on. We got through that together, we can get through this.

A

I don't understand. I mean I don't understand why she's telling me these things. I don't know what she's trying to say to me.

I don't see what it's got to do with her and me.

I don't know why she feels she wants to say all this.

I don't want to hear it now. I have my new job. I've organised all this life-change for both of us. Change is difficult. Change hurts. I think we have enough to cope with.

There's something else, something else she's leading up to, something that has its roots in *then* and has its hooks in *now*.

B

The unit was our last best hope. It was also a school for crime. Sometimes I think Angie knew all about that and sometimes not. I think she knew a good bit about it. She had this thing that she would do with the mad fucks like Bruno and Damon, where she would get them to tell the stories of their exploits over and over, until it came out that most of them were really semi-fuck-ups, as most crimes are; and she would get the boys to measure up the risks against the rewards so they could see how silly most crimes were, and how they nearly always carried lots of unintended consequences. She even used to say, sometimes, Angie, she used to say well if I can't persuade you to be straight maybe I can persuade you to be sensible.

She had it the wrong way round. Bruno and Damon *were* straight in their way, they never robbed Angie for example, but they were never sensible: they were mad fucks as a way of life, like a religion, Bruno especially. And Angie's little crime studies had unintended consequences too: a girl like me who had never done anything against the law except make love was having a whole new world of possibilities opened up to her. The mad fucks, Bruno Mick and Damon, they loved me from the start, I was their treasure and their little mascot; I adored their style and recklessness and held them in awe for their deep-down heavy criminal experience, and they were dazzled by my shiny little brain, the way I hoovered up the subjects, they were proud of me, like I was doing it for them, and it felt as if I was, a bit, after a while.

Steal from her? They would steal *for* her. She only had to mention something, like one time she said her hi-fi was buggered and did anyone know the best place to get a new one. They only had a brand new Bang & Olufsen on her table next morning all in the maker's wrappings. I never knew if she kept it or not. Little moral problem for Ange, that was. Weigh up the risks against the rewards, calculate the unintended consequences. She was interesting, Ange, there was a bit of outsider about her, too, she had a bit of a problem with authority. She liked us; she even liked Bruno.

One time not long after I'd arrived there, she took us all horsey-riding. She was always thinking up treats for us, we used to call her Auntie Ange sometimes. Go-kart racing, ice skating, rowing boats . . . None of us had ever seen a horse close up before, they looked gigantic. There was this dead strict woman there who started lecturing us on the right way to do this and the right way to do that, and all the little things we had to remember to think about before we even approached the horses, and after about thirty seconds of this, while she was still rabbiting on about posture or something, Bruno just took a run at the biggest horse of the lot, this huge ginger job, and leapt on his back. He never managed to get his feet in the stirrups at all, his legs were sticking out all ways, and he had hold of its mane, and the horse you could see was fucking furious with Bruno, and started leaping about in the yard with Bruno on his back yelling 'Come on you fucker!' like a rodeo rider, honest, you could see a foot of daylight between him and the horse when he jumped. It didn't last long, of course, about six jumps, and Bruno came off, turned over in the air, and landed on his head. We all thought he was dead, but he got up laughing. He was like that, Bruno. Never admit he was hurt. He had no fear. You could see it in his eyes, sometimes, and the first time I saw it was that afternoon. He really didn't care, Bruno. He was careless of his life. He didn't care if he lived or died.

We all learnt to ride that afternoon. Once she got over her shock and her rage at the bad Bruno, the woman was all right with us. She said I had good balance and good hands and I was like a little monkey. I didn't mind when she said that; she said it as a compliment. I think she fancied me actually. And it was good, crouched above the big horse and letting him canter, feeling all that weight shift under you and hovering over him, letting him take you. Feeling nervous, but taking a risk and trusting yourself and him. Sexy, really, like it says in the stories. But Bruno was miles the best of us, because he had no fear at all and the horses understood that. He had them jumping, flat out galloping, the lot. The woman said she'd never seen anyone learn so fast.

We were all proud of Bruno that day. King of the mad fucks. But I'd seen his crazy eyes. He didn't care if he lived or died.

A

When she tells me about it, it's as if she's back there. She even looks about fourteen years old.

I think she wants to include me in her life, but it works the other way: I feel excluded. What do I have to do with all that self-admiring shit? We're here now, not there.

Get to the point, get to the point, if there is one.

I stand on the grass in front of the cottage. I breathe the clean night air. So clean up here, the night air. I can smell the grass. Next year, I'll have roses in this little patch here protected from the sheep by this low dry-stone wall. I have been digging the turf with my new spade. The clean sound as it shears through the turf. I can smell the fresh clean smell of the earth the spade gashed. I stare out across the valley to where the dark hill looms on the other side. I like it out here. I like this silence.

Get to the point, if there is one.

B

Angie used to get a lot of interesting people down the unit: writers, painters, theatre people, movie people. Partly to broaden our horizons, partly to give us contacts that might lead to jobs, most of us being a bit on the unqualified side. These people were friends of Angie's and friends of friends, and some of them were doing it from the goodness of their hearts, but most of them I think got off on criminals, they liked a bit of rough and a bit of wild, they had a weakness for mad fucks.

That was how Bruno met Charles. Charles is a film director who, like Paul, is partial to a bit of rough and wild, though unlike Paul, Charles actually makes movies. He came and talked to us about movies and left us his video camera so we could make our own (two of the girls made this really filthy one) and then used Bruno and Mick as non-speaking players in *Softbelly*. Yeah, you can get it down the vid shop. See their faces, read their names. I will never get it out again because it makes me cry too much.

Charles fell under Bruno's spell, but not vice versa. Charles was crazy about Bruno for a while, but Bruno was too mad to be crazy about Charles, if that makes sense. He liked to be admired though, by Charles and his campy mates, and he was happy to let Charles suck his cock and give him presents and introduce him to people who would also give him small jobs and for all I know have sex with him as well. Poor Bruno, he thought he had all the power, but really he had none.

This was going before Bruno and I got started, and it went on after, in spasms, right up to when Bruno died and it was in fact what killed him . . .

In my dreams he walks towards me burning . . .

No, look, talk about something else, yeah, this, this: we had this game, me and Bruno, when we were on a tube train, if ever we found ourselves alone in an empty carriage we would have to take all our clothes off and fuck between stations, standing up, usually, braced against the sway and rattle, the black sooty pipes outside like dead snakes whistling past our faces, my back jammed hard against the doors, laughing at his crazy grin, he was always laughing when we fucked, he really loved to fuck, Bruno, and so did I, one leg up and clinging round his back like a monkey and my strong young monkey arms around his neck, and sometimes we'd cruise into the station like that, shagging like aliens from outer space, and see the pale moon faces of the astonished travellers, their eyes ablink their dumb gobs open in disbelief . . .

Deep friends, mad fucks, die for each other.

Don't look like that, I'm not telling you to hurt you, you are my dear one, you want to know all about me, you said so.

You are my deep friend now and Bruno's dead.

Charles had this car, a Scimitar like Princess Anne's, to pull the rough wild boys in, and he used to let Bruno drive around in it. (Big deal, Bruno who could steal any car he wanted.) And when they had their final row and screaming match Bruno broke a lot of stuff in Charles's flat although he never damaged Charles himself, and went off with the Scim.

And you know what Charles did? Only reported it stolen.

Bruno came straight to me. 'I've come to take you for a ride,' he said. He had been crying, first time I ever saw tears on his face, and I thought maybe he did love Charles, and I was jealous. He wouldn't talk about it though, all he would say about it was that he was finished with that fat fairy for fucking good. He was speeding on something and very agitated, and we cruised around for a while and he was driving in this wild lurchy way as if he wanted something bad to happen; and then when the police cars started to pick him up he went completely impossible, straight through three red lights at over sixty and I looked at him and he wasn't laughing, he was crying, and I thought fuck you Bruno I am not going to die because you've quarrelled with your boyfriend and I asked him to let me out, and he did, straight away. He pulled into the kerb and I opened the door.

I said: 'Bruno.'

He just stared straight ahead, both hands on the wheel, gunning the engine.

I said: 'Take care.'

He said nothing.

We were on Westbourne Park Villas. I shut the door, and just as I did that, one of the police cars came round the corner ahead, coming straight towards him. Bruno put his foot down and drove straight at it. I thought they were going to crash head on and I wanted to shut my eyes but at the last second the police driver pulled his wheel and went up the pavement and through someone's garden wall, and the Scimitar grazed by but Bruno had lost it: he sideswiped a parked van and then went straight into a lamppost.

It was like a firestorm. I could feel the heat from fifty yards away. Scimitars are made of fibreglass and every part of them burns. No chance of anybody getting near. I was trying to walk towards it though and I was trying to call out, but I could not walk and I could not speak. All you could see of the car was red flame and this huge cloud of thick black horrible smoke and this black shape inside that was Bruno.

Then this thing happened.

The door of the car opened and Bruno got out and started walking slowly towards me as if he had no idea he was on fire. Every part of him was on fire and he was on his feet and walking. He spread his arms wide, the palms towards me, as if he was showing me something. His hands and his face were black already, but his eyes, I could still see his eyes, his bright green eyes.

I can still see them.

I suppose he only walked about six steps really, before he fell down.

He was still burning, burning.

Still burning.

After a long while, Alan asked me if I'd ever had an HIV test. I said no. He got up and went outside.

After a while I went out there too. He was sitting on the wall. It was one o'clock in the morning, and so quiet it felt as though we were the only people awake in Swaledale.

He was sitting on the wall staring out across the valley, though there was nothing to see there. When I sat down by him I saw that he was crying. He started telling me some stuff about how he liked to watch me when I was asleep. The way he told it, it sounded like an accusation.

I thought: this is my dear one. We can come through this.

A

I go out, I come home. She's there. *Inside! Inside!* At night she loves me in her sleep. I wake early and watch her dreaming. We go to the pub and sit together. We don't need to talk to people. We don't need to talk to each other. We radiate the pale heat of our private sensuality. We are complete.

I understand that there were people in her past. I just don't want to hear about them. Is that unreasonable? Paul might need some help, apparently. What sort of help? No information. When will he need it? It isn't clear. Why do we owe him anything? Don't ask her why, she'll only say because.

The silence here is sometimes almost more than I can cope with.

We are husband and wife, but we are brother and sister too. She is the sister that my mother lost, the stillborn sister between me and Nick, who would have been my big sister, who would have taken care of me. She is my little sister too, my phantom little sister, and I know every fold and crevice of her little cunt, I know the shape and substance of each chromosome: we belong to each other, our love transcends all laws and statutes, they can imprison me for longer and longer sentences, but each time I am released she flies into my arms. I am her Daddy as I hold her in my strong protecting grasp, she is my Mummy as she holds her nipple to my mouth and soothes me into sleep, she is my Daddy as she drives the car and aims the gun, I am her Mummy as she steps out of the bath into the warm towel I hold for her, I am her Mummy as I give her suck. Quite simply, our love encompasses the world, and needs nothing for its completion.

So where does she go when she's asleep? Why does she keep reminding me of our separateness when I want us to be at one? What do her silences and absences betoken? *What is it that she wants of me?*

B

I've decided to just let it happen and see how it works out. Deep friends, mad fucks, die for each other. He is not a mad fuck, but the rest of it is true, I think. And because of Alan I'm becoming what I'm going to be.

Paul has been in touch.

I walked down to the garage this morning and Jim Arkright was looking out for me. He's nice, Jim Arkright. Big bald head, blue eyes like a china doll, and he always wears one of those old-fashioned lumberjack bomber jacket things with the big checks and the mock sheepskin lining. Apart from Jim Arkright the only people I've seen wearing that sort of jacket were sleeping in doorways with bottles in their hands.

'Friend of yours on the phone,' he said.

'Was he called Paul?'

'Yes. He said to tell you he was sorry but he's on his way.'

'Was that all?'

'Yes. He said to tell you he'd explain when he sees you.'

'He didn't say what time or anything?'

'No.'

'When did he phone?'

'Oh, ah, must have been about six this morning.' He blushed.

Jim sometimes spends the night in the garage with a married woman from Gunnerside, when she can get away. Everyone knows it, no one mentions it.

'Look,' I said. 'He's in a bit of bother, our friend.' I said our friend because it sounded more respectable. 'Be grateful if you didn't mention it to anyone.'

'No problem,' he said.

'We've had a fox round, going to see if we can shoot him,' I said.

'Sly buggers foxes. Want any help?'

'No, no,' I said. 'Just, you know, didn't want to worry you, if you heard any bangs or anything.'

'Won't worry me, Beatrice,' he said.

People say it's difficult to get accepted by the locals up here. I would say it is a fucking doddle.

I didn't go far from the cottage all day. I was listening for the car. I did a bit of painting on the window frames, did a bit of digging in Alan's garden bit, with his sharp new spade. See me nowadays. B. Monkey as used to be. The changed girl. The hawk was there again today, just hovering above the river.

I heard a car about four, and walked down to the garage. The garage was closed and boarded up. I walked round the corner and there was a very mucky red Sierra. Paul was sitting in the driver's seat looking terrible. I've never seen him so pale. I walked over to the car. He needed all his strength to wind the window down.

'Benny, darling,' he said. 'I know it's smart to live in the country but this is ridiculous.'

I could tell it was something he had been planning to say for hours, but now he'd finally got here he was too exhausted to get it out right.

'Benny, I'm in terrible fucking trouble I'm afraid,' he said.

'Move over,' I said. 'I'll drive you up.'

He could hardly even do that. He looked as if he was coming apart at the joints. I noticed he had a bandage on his left hand.

I booted the Sierra hard up the track, and skittered her smoothly round the hairpins, whoosh, whoosh; I needn't have bothered, Paul was too out of it to notice. He gasped, though, every time we hit a bump, so I slowed right down as we got on the grassy track and coaxed the Sierra up and then right round back of the cottage where it couldn't be seen. Easy enough because it had been dry for weeks.

He managed to get out of the car by himself and walk into the cottage but when he got in he just sat down on the sofa and stared in front of him. He wasn't taking anything in. I was irritated with him. I wanted him to see how nice we had it. We even had flowers on the table. Christ, he looked bad, though.

'Cup of tea, Dad?' He managed a little smile at that.

'Oh thank you Benny that would be lovely,' he said. 'Just like old times.'

It was, in a way. I went and put the kettle on.

'I hope you haven't come to tell me I got to go back to school,' I said, 'because I'm not going. I'm going to stay home and look after you, Dad, so save your breath.'

Just stuff from our old games. I wanted to cheer him up a bit, I couldn't bear to see him so broken down.

'What's the matter with your hand?' I asked him.

'Oh, God. Don't ask, Benny.'

'Come on,' I said, 'let's have a look.'

I started to unwrap the bandage, very carefully.

'Those chaps came back,' he said. 'They hurt me, Benny.'

His hand was a mess. At first I couldn't see what the matter with it was, then I realised they had cut the top off his middle finger.

'Oh, Paul,' I said.

'I know,' he said. 'How am I going to play the piano now?'

He met my eye. I tried to keep a straight face, but I had to smile, and so did he, then. We both knew what the other one was thinking: that finger was the one he liked to stroke me with.

'You did pay them, Paul,' I said.

'No, I didn't,' he said. 'Animals like that. I have my pride. I was to meet them today at ten, but I didn't show. Animals like that. They can fucking whistle for it.'

'Shit, Paul,' I said. 'You're a mad fuck, you know that?'

He smiled. Lovely smile. I'll always remember his smile.

'They don't know where you've gone, do they?' I said.

'No,' he said. And then, after a while, 'I don't think so.'

A

When I got back from school he was there, sitting on the sofa, in a white shirt, just like before, and a bandage on his left hand. Beatrice had lit a fire, but he was shivering a bit. He looked ill, but just as contemptuously at ease as he had looked in his own hot smoky flat. He had a glass of wine in his right hand and a cigarette burning in an ashtray.

'Hello, Alan,' he said, without getting up or even moving. 'It's good to see you.'
   'What are you doing here?' I said. I didn't feel like being friendly.
   'I'm sorry. Bit of an emergency. I'll try not to be too much of a nuisance.' He smiled.

Beatrice came in from the kitchen. She looked guilty, like a little girl who's been stealing someone else's crisps out of their schoolbag.
   'Sorry, Alan,' she said. 'Paul's in a spot. You don't mind, do you?'
   'Yes I do, actually,' I said. 'Why does he have to come here?'
   'He just has to,' she says.
   'Oh, tell him,' said Paul.

So I sat down and she told me. While she told me I just sat there looking at Paul as he sat on my sofa smoking his cigarette. He's like a stain on my sofa, I thought. He's like that stain on the sofa in my dreams, that was more than a stain, that was like a gangrene, rotting the sofa, infecting the plants. He's staining my marriage, I thought; he's rotting my life.

Drugs. Drug takers, drug dealers. I hate drugs. I hate druggy people. I don't even like to be drunk. I hate that loss of control, that imbecilic euphoria of the self-deceived. I wanted to throw him out. But he was begging for shelter. And Beatrice loved him once and clearly feels she owes him. That she could have once loved a man like Paul is part of the spreading stain, but something I cannot deal with now.

About one thing we all agreed: if these people know where Paul is, they are going to come, and if they come, they're going to come soon.

The shotgun is loaded, both barrels. We know how to use it. Surely if they see it they will be deterred.

At dusk, we heard sounds at the front of the cottage, rough quick steps in the tussocky grass, what sounded like heavy breathing.

Only the hedgehog. She has been coming, at dusk, with her children, for a few weeks now. Hedgehogs are armed, they don't care who hears them. Beatrice went outside with a saucer of milk. She left the door open. Paul was still sitting on the sofa, steadily filling the ashtray with his stinking butts. I was sitting on a hard chair opposite him, facing the door. I could not bear to think that she had made love with this man. I couldn't take my eyes off his thin fingers with the brown nicotine stains as he stubbed out another cigarette. I couldn't stop imagining his thin fingers paddling in her vagina.

Outside she was a graceful silhouette against the darkening sky, stooping to lay down the saucer of milk for the hedgehog family. It was so quiet we could hear the river.

And a single car, distant, coming closer.

I went out and stood by Beatrice. The car was still miles away. But getting closer all the time. It might mean anything or nothing. Whoever was driving wasn't using headlights. That might mean someone local who knew the road well: Jim

Arkright always drove on sidelights, to save the battery, he said. But as it got closer it didn't sound like Jim's car at all. It was a big quiet car, big engine. We heard whoever it was stop by the garage, and switch off the engine. We couldn't see anything because of the curve of the hill.

'If it's them, they're walking up,' she said. 'I'll get the gun.'

'I'll get it,' I said.

I went into the house and got it. Checked that it was loaded, both barrels.

'Kill them for me, Alan,' said Paul as I walked past him. I felt like turning the gun on him.

I went out to Beatrice. She was standing by the wall, not right in front of the cottage, but further down the track, where I had staked out a patch for vegetables. If it was them, and they were walking up, we had plenty of time. It takes me eight minutes and I am very fit.

'Look,' she said. 'These people are killers, Alan. What we do is this: we get down behind the wall. I'll tell you if it's them, and if it is, wait till they get so close you can't miss, then stand up and shoot them in the middle of the chest.'

I started to shake. I couldn't believe what I was hearing.

'Jesus,' I said. 'Is this what you do?'

'I've never done it before,' she said. 'I will, though.'

'I can't,' I said. 'Not like that. I can't. I won't.'

'Give me the gun then,' she said. She snatched it off me.

'It's all right, Alan,' she said. 'You don't know them. They're not just coming for Paul, they're coming for me.'

She was breathing deeply, great deep breaths through her nose. 'We'll get them,' she whispered. 'Get down now. I can hear them.'

I could hear them now too. They weren't talking, but their breath was louder than their footsteps on the turf. It was a stiff climb. Then I saw them, surreal in their square sharp suits against the round hill. They weren't looking to either side, just plodding steadily up towards the cottage. One tall man and one short broad man. The tall one was limping slightly. He had a stiff leg. I glanced at Beatrice and she nodded. I started to feel extremely strange. I felt a desperate urge to have something to protect myself, and, absurdly, pulled out one of the sticks I'd used to mark the vegetable patch. The two men were closer now. Beatrice put her hand on my arm. Then she stood up, and, stupidly, so did I. The men turned, surprised. They were only about ten feet away. The tall one started to say something, and Beatrice shot him in the chest. He sat down immediately and then pitched over sideways. The other one turned and tried to run, and she shot him in the back. He fell down immediately too, and lay twitching. The tall one was very still. His face was half hidden in the deep tyre track, but I could see his eyes and mouth were wide open. My ears were still ringing from the shotgun blast. I couldn't seem to get my breath properly, as if I had been shot myself.

Beatrice scrambled over the wall and stood over the short man. She lifted the gun, as if to smash the butt into his head. I tried to speak, to say, please, enough, leave him . . . she bent over him, then straightened.

'I think it's all right,' she said.

The man was lying still now.

Then something made us both turn back towards the cottage.

Paul was standing in the doorway. He was swaying, holding on to the doorpost.

She said: 'It's OK Paul, we got them. They're both dead. Are you all right?'

He said: 'Well, no, I'm not, actually.'

His voice sounded strange, weak and somehow gurgly, as if he was gargling, for a joke. Then he bent his knees, and went down very gently, hardly making a sound, and another man came out of the cottage.

I heard Beatrice behind me breathe in sharply. The man stepped over Paul's body and peered at us. It was getting darker all the time. I couldn't make his face out.

'Stay there,' said Beatrice, 'or I'll fucking kill you too.'

'You wish, hen,' he said. 'You've done both barrels.' He had a quiet, hoarse voice, and a thick Scottish accent. He looked at me.

'And who the fuck are you?' he said. I didn't say anything.

He seemed very relaxed, very calm, very deliberate, like a doctor or a lawyer. A professional man.

'Ah, what the fuck,' he said. 'I don't suppose it matters.'

He took a pistol out of his pocket and aimed it at me. I couldn't move. I couldn't speak.

He pulled the trigger. Nothing happened.

'Would you fucking well believe that?' he said. He sounded mildly irritated. 'I've got a knife here somewhere, wait a minute.'

I watched him fumble in his pocket. Still I couldn't seem to move. Then I realised I was still holding the stick. It was something. I could try to keep him off. Beatrice might get away, even reload, if I could keep him at arm's length. Anything rather than stand there while he plunged the cold knife into my body. He had the knife out now. I went into the on-guard position, the stake extended as in épée, the sharp point trained on his eyes.

'Ah, for fuck's sake,' he said. 'This isnae a game.'

'Come on,' I said. I was starting to feel better.

He came forward much more quickly than I expected. I lunged and the sharp point jabbed him in the cheek, he grabbed for the stick but couldn't hold on, I jumped back out of range, on guard again. The adrenalin was flowing now, I felt hot and fierce and good and keen to kill the man, whoever he was.

'Come on,' I said, and he lunged forward again. I leaned to the left and hit inside his attack, a clean hit to the middle of the target, but he kept on coming, he was too strong, he was terribly strong, it had all gone wrong, I could smell his breath, and then Beatrice came from behind him and swung the edge of the spade into his head. He stood still, looking puzzled. Then blood gushed down over his face like a red curtain, and he toppled forward on to his knees. Then on to his face.

And then it was quiet again.

And we stared at each other, Beatrice and I, for a long time.

A

When I think about that time now, I cannot believe what we did. I want to forget it, it was not heroic, it was banal and exhausting, and terribly, terribly hard work, and it was sort of . . . *evil*, I think, in a way. We worked all night, longing for sleep, and it was like working in sleep, for me, the darkness, the terrible weight and awkwardness of the huge wrapped shapes . . . I think we used the big car, the Granada, but we could only get it so far up.

So quiet, under the stars. The little night animals scurrying. An owl, hunting, that we never saw. I keep remembering the sound she made as she came up behind the man she said was David Smith that last time and split his skull. It was a terrible sound, an animal sound, not like a human sound at all. She saved my life, I suppose, but when I think about it, sometimes I think I would rather have died than heard that sound.

Afterwards, she said she was sorry.

I don't know what she meant, exactly.

And since then, nothing. No one seems to have seen them, no one has come looking for them. They seem to have been people that no one wanted. Both the cars were hire cars. We drove to Darlington and left the Granada in a pub car park, then drove the Sierra to York and left it at the railway station.

They dig for peat up here still, but not six feet deep. They're not supposed to do that, even. This is a National Park. Protected area.

We seem to be quite safe.

I don't think I can handle it. Beatrice seems to be able to handle it easily, but I don't think I can. I keep remembering something Rupert said in the gym, just after the first time I saw Beatrice with the two boys. He said, as if it was simple, as if it explained everything: well, I think they're criminals, you see.

And she has changed, a bit. These days, when I come home, she doesn't rush into my arms; she tends to look at me anxiously, then come to me slowly. She says she is fine but she worries about me. We sit together in the pub and I am not sure what we radiate. Occasionally I look at her across the room and think: she's actually quite ordinary to look at. Sometimes her astonishing smile simply looks vacant and greedy.

I can't bear what seems to be happening.

B

B. Monkey.

Being good now.

This time I've cracked it.

No more Fucknose.

It was horrible horrible but it had to be done. I am sorry Alan had to be dragged into it but glad in a way too for him to see it and be part of it and be there when I changed, because he has saved me really and I saved him a bit too.

I do think about Paul, but the more I think about Paul the more I realise he was cruising for death. No one will remember him as tenderly as I do, but I don't yearn tragically for him. When you are really through something you know it, don't you.

It's OK. It's OK. Everything is going to be OK.

A

Three months now.

It isn't getting better, it is worse.

I can't explain it to her. We have silences, and distances, and absences.

I could say: one time, I went up the stairs and opened the door to my room on the second floor, she turned from the window, a J-cloth in her hand . . .

Where does it go, when it's gone?

I've been awake for hours, watching her sleep. On her back with one hand flung behind her head, the little dark ringlet of hair in her armpit. Her dark eyelids, darker than the olive of her cheeks, her thick dark lashes. When she dreams her eyelids tremble almost imperceptibly but very quickly, and her mouth moves too, slowly, clumsily, druggily, trying to keep up. I wonder where she is, who she is, who she is with . . . I feel sick, and weary.

Where does it go?

I am a great success at the school. The parents showered me with gifts at end of term. I have a disciple there. Her name is Alison. It's just her second year of teaching. She has asked if we could team-teach together. She's thin, dark, quiet, intelligent. We have a lot in common.

Beatrice is dreaming again. Her clumsy mouth trying to follow her racing brain. Little glimpses of her teeth. Little glimpses of the whites of her eyes. Her steady breathing. Her steady heartbeat. I realise that tears are rolling down my cheeks.

Where does it go, when it's gone? What can we trust?

B

The water's warm, and deep, a lovely dark green, and it's just like I hoped, I can breathe and talk under the water, we are all swimming along together under the water with the fishes, and I know it's a dream, and real as well, and Mick's there, and Damon, and Bruno, Bruno's got those raggy denim shorts he had, all clinging to him, pale as a fish, and all whole again, not a mark on him, and Damon is up ahead of us and he turns round smiling, and I'm telling them my news, but it's hard to talk properly under water, it comes out all bubbly, and they start to laugh, and I'm laughing too, and saying I'm going to have a baby, I'm going to have a baby, a bubbababy, a bubbabubbababy, and I can't stop laughing, I'm so happy, I feel so very strong and happy, and I am swimming away from them now, thrusting up and away with strong strokes, up towards the light, up out of my sleep, to where my dear one waits for me.